DAN FREEDMAN

Quiz No 212832
The Kick Off

Freedman, Dan
B.L.: 4.9
Points: 4.0   MY

📖 SCHOLASTIC

First published in the UK in 2007 by Scholastic Children's Books
An imprint of Scholastic Ltd
Euston House, 24 Eversholt Street
London, NW1 1DB, UK
Registered office: Westfield Road, Southam, Warwickshire, CV47 0RA
SCHOLASTIC and associated logos are trademarks and or registered trademarks of
Scholastic Inc.

This edition published by Scholastic Ltd, 2012

ISBN 978 1407 11613 6

A CIP catalogue record for this book is available from the British Library

Printed and bound by CPI Group (UK) Ltd, Croydon, CR0 4YY
Papers used by Scholastic Children's Books are made from wood
grown in sustainable forests.

16

www.scholastic.co.uk/zone

Acknowledgements

Thanks to:

Mum and Ivan for your support – always.
Dad, Linda, Liz and Sam too.
Jenny Parrott, Kate Paice and Ena McNamara for pointing me in the right direction.
Hazel Ruscoe; this story is inspired by the ideas we had together.
Grandpa for sharing with me your love of words.
Dawn Scott and John Allpress at The FA for the technical advice on the drills.
Caspian Dennis for making it all happen, and to the whole team at Scholastic for your tremendous support and commitment to me and the project.
And to Lola for your amazing belief and never letting me give up. How did you know, right from the start?

Part
One

The Trial

Friday 21 July – Last Day of Term

KINGFIELD SCHOOL
UNDER 14s TRIAL MATCH
60:00 MINS PLAYED
BLUES 1   **REDS 0**
WALSH, 22

This was it. This was Jamie's chance to prove himself. This was what he'd waited six months for. Kingfield School didn't know who Jamie Johnson really was. They didn't know the kind of talent he had.

Now he could show them.

Dillon Simmonds had no idea who he'd been messing with. Jamie could shove all his stupid words back down his big, fat, spotty mouth with one goal today.

That was the plan anyway. But these trials to see who would be in the Kingfield Under-fourteen A team next year were not going according to the script.

When he most needed his skills, nothing was working for Jamie.

There were only ten minutes left and Jamie hadn't shown a thing.

People kept hoofing the ball to him in the air. He was never going to get anywhere like that. He was a winger. He needed the ball passed to his feet.

Jamie had been in pain since the first minute, too. He was wearing a pair of worn-out old socks that had holes in them and his boots were rubbing against his heels the whole time. He'd scored some of his best ever goals in these boots, but today they were hurting him. They had sawn off all the skin on the backs of his heels. He was sure he was bleeding.

Jamie bent down and undid his laces. Maybe if he re-tied them looser it wouldn't hurt as much.

He had just done up his laces and was getting ready to stand up and get back into the game when he suddenly felt a knee jar right into his ribs. It knocked him sideways on to the ground.

"Oi, Ginger Minger – what you doing on the floor?

Had enough, have you?" sneered Dillon Simmonds as he jogged past. They both knew full well that it was him who'd knocked Jamie over, and that he'd done it on purpose. You could see it in his evil smile.

"Shut your face, Simmonds – you fat numpty," said Jamie, getting to his feet.

Jamie knew that Dillon wasn't really fat. He was pretty much all muscle. But he also knew that Dillon hated being called fat so it was a good way to wind him up.

"Talk to me when you've actually touched the ball, Ginge," Dillon shouted back, laughing as he went.

Jamie jogged back to his position on the left wing. He was shaking his head. The sad thing was, for once in his life Dillon actually had a point. Jamie had hardly touched the ball all game and he knew it. Mr Marsden probably didn't even know he was on the pitch.

But then, out of nothing, it happened. A chance!

The goalkeeper on Jamie's side belted the ball forward. It was a huge kick and when it hit the hard dusty ground, it bounced so high that it went over the whole of the opposition defence.

Jamie spotted what was going to happen before anyone else on the pitch. He dashed after the ball and was way too quick for any of the defenders to keep up with him.

It was just him against the keeper. He was in.

Latching on to the ball, he steadied himself as he waited for it to drop.

One sweet strike from his left foot. Then Marsden would know who Jamie Johnson was, all right.

He could have smashed it on the half-volley but he let the ball bounce to give himself that bit more time.

Then he swivelled and, with his right foot planted in the ground and his left knee bent all the way back, he got ready to snap through the strike. He wanted to rifle it into the net.

But, just as he was about to crack the ball home, he was hit by a cyclone of a challenge.

Dillon Simmonds, a human truck, had driven straight into Jamie, catapulting him into the air. Jamie found himself lying winded on the ground. His dream goal had been ripped away from him.

"Get up, you diver," shouted Dillon, grabbing Jamie's shirt by the collar.

"Get your hands off me," said Jamie, desperately trying to get his breath back.

Jamie wanted to knock him out but inside he was struggling just to breathe. Dillon had taken him out good and proper. It felt like someone was in his chest, strangling his lungs. The more he tried to gulp in the air, the more it hurt.

"OK, you two. Break it up," said Mr Marsden, who was quickly on the scene. "I saw what happened.

"You didn't make contact with the ball, Dillon – only the man. It's a penalty for the Reds."

Marsden handed Jamie the ball.

2

On the Spot

Jamie looked around. Everyone else was just staring back at him. None of the others on his team had made a move to take the penalty. It had to be him.

Jamie knew it wasn't just the keeper that he was up against now. It was every other player on the pitch. No one wanted him to score – not even his own teammates. Why would they? It was their trial too and they all wanted to get into the A team just as badly as he did. Why would they want him to steal all the glory in the last minute?

Jamie reached down and placed the ball on the spot. At first a bump in the ground made the ball roll off the spot. So Jamie picked the ball back up and stamped down hard on the spot to try and flatten it out. He could feel his heart thudding as he put the ball back down.

"Good luck, muppet," said Dillon, standing right between Jamie and the goal. He was so close that Jamie could see the little droplets of spit coming out of his stinking mouth as he spoke. "Make sure you don't MISS," he hissed.

Jamie fended Dillon's heavy frame out of the way. He needed to concentrate.

But it was hard. He wanted to be decisive but he was aware of the doubts sprouting up everywhere in his mind. Thousands of questions were all closing in on him at once: Power or placement? To the side? It might go wide. Straight down the middle? The keeper will save it.

Mr Marsden raised the whistle to his mouth. The burst of noise was the signal for Jamie to step forward.

"I can't miss, I can't miss," he said to himself as he walked towards the spot, head bowed.

And then everything went completely blank.

Jamie saw his feet run up to the ball but somehow he felt unable to control them. His mind and body were disconnected from each other. He was taking the penalty but he had no idea what he was actually going to do with it.

Then something very unlucky happened.

As Jamie moved to strike the ball with his left foot, his right foot went over a divot in the pitch, twisting his ankle right over.

It threw Jamie off balance completely. He started to fall over. He should have stopped, got himself together and taken another run-up. But he didn't. He still tried to take the penalty.

As he was falling to the ground, he flung his foot towards the ball so desperately, so violently, that his left boot actually flew off his foot.

It shot right up into the air.

Jamie yelled out in horror.

His boot rocketed skywards, doing somersaults as it went. Meanwhile, the ball that should have been flying into the back of the net was rolling slowly and painfully along the ground towards the goalkeeper's waiting hands.

Jamie could not believe it. This was his worst nightmare.

He started to hear something behind him. It was laughter. He turned around and saw that all the players on both sides were laughing. At him.

"That's the worst penalty I've ever seen! You're rubbish!" Dillon shouted, pointing straight at Jamie. "And this ginger minger thinks he can play for the A's!"

Jamie's blood was boiling with rage, embarrassment and frustration. The sight and sound of Dillon's stupid, ugly, disgusting laugh was too much to take.

He shoved Dillon hard in the chest and walked away.

"Aaah," cried Dillon dramatically. He stumbled backwards and fell to the ground clutching his neck.

Jamie couldn't believe what Dillon was doing. He was actually faking it. He was pretending Jamie had punched him!

"Aaah, ref!" protested Dillon, rolling on the ground in apparent agony. "He's done me, ref."

"Johnson, come here," said Marsden, beckoning Jamie with his finger. His voice was serious.

"You're not falling for that, are you, sir? He's taking the—"

"I'm not falling for anything." Marsden reached for his pocket.

"Sir! He's trying to con you. I didn't do anything!"

"Yes, you did, Jamie. I know you're upset about the penalty but you raised your hands to an opponent and you can't do that on a football pitch."

Marsden brandished the red card above his head so everyone could see.

Jamie had been sent off.

KINGFIELD SCHOOL
UNDER 14s TRIAL MATCH
FULL-TIME RESULT

BLUES 1	REDS 0
WALSH. 22	JOHNSON MISSED PEN. 61
	JOHNSON SENT OFF. 62

As he trudged off, Jamie tried for the millionth time to work out why it was that Dillon hated him so much. Maybe it was because Jamie was new at Kingfield. He'd only joined the school in January. Before that, he'd been at The Grove, the other big school in the area and Kingfield's fiercest rivals.

Dillon despised The Grove. Jamie knew that much because they had played football against each other every year that Jamie had been at The Grove. It had always seemed like Dillon had been on a personal mission to kick lumps out of every single Grove player in every match they had played. The Grove were a good football school, though, and Jamie had been one of their top players. In last year's match between Kingfield and The Grove Jamie had scored twice and The Grove had won 3 – 1. Maybe that was the real reason that Dillon kept trying to slate Jamie.

But it wasn't Jamie's fault that he used to go to The Grove. He'd only gone there because that's where his mum had gone and she'd wanted him to go to the same school.

He'd actually been wanting to join Kingfield for ages. Not only was it much nearer to Jamie's house but Jack Marshall – Jamie's best mate – went there too. For years Jamie had begged his mum to allow him to go to Kingfield and, finally, last October, Jamie's mum had given in and said he could join.

When they'd found out that there was a space for him to start in January, Jamie had jumped at the chance, even if it was in the middle of the school year. Jamie's mum wasn't so sure but in the end she'd allowed it, on the condition that his school work didn't suffer.

Jamie had been so excited to start and to be at the same school as Jack, but life as a new boy at Kingfield hadn't been as easy as he'd thought.

Most people already had their group of friends. It was difficult for Jamie to get on with them. Sometimes he'd got into a bit of trouble on purpose, just to get noticed by the others. Plus he'd had Dillon on his case the whole time too. It had started right from Jamie's very first day, when Dillon had said that Jamie couldn't play in the football match during break.

Football was what had made Jamie popular at The Grove and he needed it to do the same for him at Kingfield. He'd waited months for the day to come when he could show Kingfield that he'd got some serious talent. He wanted people to go around the school talking about how good he was. He wanted to hear people talking next to their lockers about how fast he could sprint and how he could go around any defender. He wanted all the teachers to know that he was the best left winger in the school. And, most of all, he wanted some respect.

Instead, what he had was twenty-one other boys laughing at how he had taken the worst penalty in the history of football. Great. Just great.

Jamie was the first out of the changing room after the game. He hated the communal showers. All the other boys were already starting to look like men. Jamie still looked like a scrawny boy. He was one of the youngest in the year too; he'd only turned thirteen in June.

But today he had even more reason than normal not to want to stick around in the changing room too long. The others had stopped laughing now, but just looking at everyone was enough to remind Jamie what a fool he'd made of himself. He had to get away.

Jamie kicked the changing-room door open and stomped out. Two of the boys he'd become mates with, Tesh Prashad and Ollie Walsh, weren't far behind. Ollie was the one who'd scored the only goal in the trials. He was lucky – that goal had already booked him his spot in the A's for next year. Tesh would be in the B's, same as usual.

"You coming down the bus shelter?" asked Tesh as they left the school gates. "We're going to get some grub from the newsagent's and then pick up the bikes."

"Some of the girls are coming down," said Ollie, putting his arm around Jamie's shoulder. "You should call Jack."

Ollie and Tesh were happy. Of course they were. It was the last day of term. The summer holidays were just about to start.

Jamie should've been happy too. But he wasn't. He felt like he hated everyone – even his mates. Most of all, though, he was angry with himself. He'd expected so much from himself. He'd really built the trials up in his mind. And then he'd delivered nothing. Less than nothing.

"Nah, I've got stuff to do," he said, wriggling himself free. He wasn't in the mood for the bus shelter.

3

A New Friend

Jamie only wanted to talk to one person.

Jamie's granddad seemed to be the only one in the whole world who didn't give Jamie any grief. He never told him what to do. Jamie couldn't stand being told what to do.

But when it came to football, Mike Johnson certainly knew what he was talking about. The Hawkstone United "Young Player of the Year" award that he'd won three seasons in a row forty years ago were all the qualifications he needed to gain Jamie's respect.

They both loved the Hawks and the fact that his grand-dad had played for them made him a legend in Jamie's eyes. When Jamie's dad had left home, Jamie's mum changed both of their surnames back to her maiden name of Johnson. The older he got, the more proud Jamie felt that he had the same name as his granddad.

It wasn't like Jamie's granddad was trying to replace Jamie's dad. It was more that he was always there if Jamie needed him. They were friends as much as they were family, and he'd even asked Jamie to call him Mike rather than Granddad because he'd said that being called Granddad would make him feel like a right old pensioner.

Everyone said that had it not been for the knee injury, Jamie's granddad could have gone on to become one of the best players in Hawks history. Mike still took Jamie to see the Hawks play as often as he could, and when he sat next to Mike at the ground, Jamie always dreamed that one day he would be on the pitch playing for Hawkstone and Mike would be in the stands to see him do it. If he had the opportunity to make one wish in his life come true, that would be the one he would choose.

"Anyone can miss a penalty, JJ," said Mike.

Jamie had just told him what had happened. He'd taken the long route back from school through the park. He'd thought it might give him time to think of some positives from the trial. But it hadn't worked. Jamie couldn't remember one good thing he'd done in the whole game.

"The important thing is that you have the confidence to step up and take the next one when it comes along. Football is about balls, after all."

"I know," said Jamie. "But this is more than just a mistake. I'm never gonna get in the A team now. I'll be lucky to get in the C team, I reckon."

"Hang on a minute, Jamie," said Mike, shaking his head. "The season hasn't even started yet and you're already writing yourself off, are you? The C team? You? Come on!"

"You didn't see it, Mike. It was so embarassing."

"It's irrelevant, Jamie. It's gone. What you need to do is keep your mind positive and stick at it. If everyone got what they wanted just by clicking their fingers, nothing would be worth wanting, would it?"

"Well, I don't know. . ."

"Jamie, are you good enough to get into the A's?"

"I think so."

"You *think* so?"

"OK, yeah. I *am* good enough. I'm as good as any of them."

"Right, and you've got the whole of the holidays ahead of you now. So if you want to get in this team, then make it happen."

"How do I do that, then?"

"I suggest you go back to the beginning. Let's go outside."

They went out to the small garden at the back of the house.

"Wait here for a sec," said Mike, walking to the shed at the bottom of the garden. He moved slowly. He'd walked with a limp ever since the operations he'd had on his knee when he was younger.

The shadows were starting to lengthen now. Jamie looked at how massive his was on the garden fence. He wondered how tall he would be when he grew up.

When he came back, Mike was carrying something behind his back.

"What's this?" he said, presenting a football to Jamie.

"Don't you start," Jamie snapped. "I had a bad game but I still know what a football is."

Jamie reached to grab the ball.

But Mike held on tightly.

"Ah, but if you want to be a real player, JJ, this has to be more than a football. It has to be your friend. From what you're telling me, it's not your friend at the moment."

"What? My friend?" Jamie laughed. "How can a ball be my friend?"

"How do you make friends with anyone, Jamie? Spend some time together."

Mike handed the ball over.

"And make sure you use both feet, JJ. That right foot's

not just for standing on!" he said, giving Jamie a wink as he went inside.

Jamie stood there.

All he had for company was a ball and a brick wall.

It was all he needed.

4
Home

"Jamie, where have you been?" demanded Karen Johnson, as soon as he got in.

"Nowhere – what's the problem?"

Jamie pushed his way past his mum to get a drink from the fridge. He didn't need any hassle from her. She wouldn't understand anyway. She didn't know anything about football.

"The problem is, it's nine o'clock and school finished at three and I haven't heard a word from you – that's the problem! I cook you dinner and you don't even bother to turn up. Why didn't you call me to tell me where you were?"

Jamie looked at his watch. It was 8.50. He hadn't even realized. He must have been kicking the ball against the wall for more than three hours. Not that he was in the mood to apologize for being late. Even now, he was still fuming about the match.

"I've eaten," he barked. "And why do you have to know where I am the whole time, anyway? I'm thirteen years old. I can do what I want."

"Who do you think you are?" his mum shouted back, tipping his cold dinner into the bin. "How dare you speak to me like that? The reason I bought you a phone is so that you can let me know where you are. If you aren't going to do that, then I'll take it—"

"All right! For God's sake!" said Jamie. "If you must know, I had the worst day at school *ever* and then I went to see Mike. Satisfied now?"

Jamie pounded up the stairs to his room. All he wanted was to be left alone and not to be bothered the whole time. Was that too much to ask?

He flicked on the radio. It was nearly time for the sports bulletin and he wanted to see if there had been any big-money transfers. He loved transfers. He could remember exactly how much all the Hawks players had cost when they'd been bought and which club they had joined from.

As he listened to the headlines, he headed a sponge ball against his bedroom wall, which was filled with posters of all of Jamie's favourite players.

When the bulletin had finished, Jamie switched off the radio and sat on the edge of his bed. He tumbled the ball between his hands and thought about the chat he'd had with Mike. He was right. If Jamie worked at it enough, he could still get that place in the A team. This wasn't over yet. Not by a long way.

Jack

Saturday 22 July

At 11.45 the next morning, Jamie stretched out his arms, let out a big old yawn and got up. It was time for *Sports Saturday*.

He pulled his duvet down from upstairs and perched himself on the settee with a bowl of cereal and some ice-cold milk. His mum worked at the hospital on Saturdays and Jamie enjoyed his slobby start to the weekend, feasting on the latest sports action, with the house completely to himself. During the football season he recorded all the goals while he watched them so he could go back later and watch the Hawks goals again in slow-motion.

Jamie was supposed to do some shopping for his mum this afternoon but practically as soon as the programme finished, Jamie heard the sound of a ball bouncing outside the front door.

Jack was obviously ready for their weekly kick-around at Sunningdale Park and football beat shopping any day! They had planned a long session today because it was the only chance they were going to get. Jack was visiting family in Antigua for the whole of the summer holidays.

Jack and Jamie had been best mates since they were five. They had kicked a ball around for the first time in the same week that Jack had moved into Jamie's road, about eight years ago. Since then, they had pretty much grown up together and Jamie knew that, if he needed to, he could talk to Jack about anything.

Jack was really clever and always gave good advice. Maybe if Jack had been at the trials and had been able to calm Jamie down, everything would have been different. Jamie might even have scored the penalty.

But Jack hadn't been allowed to play in the trials. Neither of them could understand why. They played together the whole time outside of school so what was the difference? As far as Jamie was concerned, Jack was by far the best goalkeeper he knew.

So what if she was a girl? She was still a great keeper.

The boys at school said Jack was fit and Jamie knew

she had a pretty face, but to him she was just a mate. A best mate.

Halfway through their jog to Sunningdale Park, Jamie suddenly came to a halt.

"What's up?" said Jack. "Run out of gas already? You need to get your fitness levels up, mate"

"Jack," said Jamie tentatively. "We're mates, right?"

"Errr . . . I think so!" said Jack sarcastically.

"Can I ask you a question, then?"

"Jamie, if you're trying to ask me out, can you just get on with it – we haven't got all day!"

"Shut up for a second, Jack. This is serious."

"OK, sorry. What is it?"

"Do I – I –" he stammered. "I mean . . . what do you think of my hair?"

"It's all right," said Jack, sizing him up. "Looks the same as normal to me."

"It *is* the same as normal, but what do you think of it? Is it really rubbish that it's . . . ginger?"

"I thought you always said that it was strawberry blond, Jamie," Jack teased.

"Just answer the question, Jack."

"Listen," said Jack, putting her face near to Jamie's so that her dreadlocks almost touched his forehead. "Your hair is cool and you're a good looking bloke. You know that, so stop trying to make me big you up. Now can we please go and play some football?"

"Yeah, cool," said Jamie, doing his best to keep a cheeky smile from flickering across his mouth.

After their kick-around, they went back to Jack's to chill and watch a film. Jamie didn't stay too late though, as Jack's flight was at 7 a.m. the next morning and she hadn't even finished packing properly.

When he left, Jamie felt a bit sad. The whole time he'd known her, they had never been apart for six weeks. That was a long time but at least they'd agreed that they would definitely meet up the night Jack got back, which was the day before school started.

He was going to miss her. Normally, they spent the whole of the summer holidays together. This time it was going to be different.

6

Park Life

If there *was* one good thing about Jack being away, though, maybe it was that now Jamie had even more time to spend with his new best friend – the ball.

For the next week, Jamie spent every single day down at Sunningdale . . . alone, just him and the ball.

He did everything he could to get to know it. He juggled it, he dribbled it, he swerved it and he curled it.

He thought about what all the best players had in common. It was the fact that they were so comfortable with the ball that they hardly ever had to look at it. They had the ball under such close control that they could lift their heads up and see the picture of what was happening all over the pitch.

That's how good Jamie wanted to be when he went

back to Kingfield. He wanted to get so close to the ball that no one would ever be able to separate them. Together, they could get him into the A team.

But soon there was a problem with the relationship. Jamie's attentions started to be drawn elsewhere.

Every day, on the pitch right next to where Jamie was practising, the same group of boys came and played a match of their own.

Although he tried to concentrate on his own routines, Jamie found himself spending more and more time watching their game instead of working on his control.

None of them knew who Jamie was but he knew who all of them were. They were the Kingfield First Eleven squad and they were doing their pre-season training.

It was weird; it was like Jamie was being hypnotized. He *had* to watch them.

It wasn't surprising though. On one pitch was a squad – including Danny Miller, the best player in the whole school – who were testing themselves to the limit in a fast-paced, competitive training session. Whereas on the next was Jamie, by himself, kicking the ball into an empty net.

They were sixteen and were cool. Jamie was thirteen and looked like he had no mates.

It was no contest.

Caught Talking

Tuesday 1 August

Just sitting there watching Danny Miller and Co. do their thing wasn't going to improve Jamie's game though.

He knew he had to concentrate on himself, not the Firsts. Somehow, he needed to make his sessions more exciting – like theirs.

So he started to commentate on himself while he practised. It made it seem so much more real.

Each day he picked a different footballer and imagined he was them when he played. He tried to take on their characteristics and dribble and shoot like they did.

Sometimes he pretended he was one of the Hawks players and other times he imagined himself as one of the big international stars. Thinking he was the best helped to make Jamie play better. It was as if their skills were being pumped into his body.

On this particular day, Jamie had decided he was going to pretend to be someone a little closer to home. He was looking forward to it.

"*Here's Danny Miller . . . he's picked this one up well inside his own half,*" Jamie started, putting on his commentator's voice as he powered down the pitch, the ball at his feet.

"*He's going through the gears now . . . he's got real pace this boy . . . the defenders can't stay with him. . .*"

So taken in was he by his own imagination, that Jamie was beginning to shout louder and louder the closer he got to the goal. He felt like he was playing in a real game and he was the star of the show.

"*Oh, a beautiful trick by Miller on the edge of the box now . . . he's made himself a yard of space. What's he going to do now?*

"*Is Miller going to have a crack?. . . He is, you know!. . . GOOOOAAAAAAAAL!*"

Jamie lingered over the word "goal" like the Brazilian commentators. He even thought he heard fans cheering his goal. He was just about to give them a wave when he realized . . . they *were* real claps.

And they were coming from behind him.

Jamie closed his eyes and listened as the claps started to turn into laughter – at first quiet, then roaring howls of derision.

Jamie turned around to see all of the First Eleven boys on the next pitch collapsing in stitches. They must have seen the whole thing.

"DANNY MILLER GOOOOAAAAAAAAL," they repeated, mimicking him.

Jamie was almost sick on the spot.

"You better watch out, Danny," shouted one of the biggest of them, "I think he's got his eye on you!"

Jamie didn't know what was more embarrassing, this or the trials the other day. At least one day he might have the chance to put the penalty miss right.

But this! What could he do about this?

The whole of the First Eleven now thought he was some kind of sad weirdo with a crush on Danny Miller. They could easily go back and tell everyone at Kingfield or, worse still, Marsden. He could add that to the ever-growing list of reasons why he'd never pick Jamie for the A's.

Time was running out for Jamie. One month. That's all he had left. How was he going to transform his game in one month? And when were people going to stop laughing at him?

8

By the Book

Wednesday 2 August

Jamie could hear Mike's knee clicking as they climbed the stairs.

He had been on crutches for six months after his injury. These days, players can come back from knee ligament injuries as good as new. But for Mike, his career was over before it had even begun.

Jamie had told Mike that he wasn't getting anywhere. That he needed help. Something to get his confidence back and make him into the player he knew he could be.

Mike had said he had something which might help.

They went into Mike's bedroom. Mike was still breathing heavily from walking up the stairs. Because his knee was hurting more and more these days, he didn't get much exercise.

There were still pictures of him and Jamie's nan on the window sill. It made Jamie really sad to think of Mike living on his own now after being married for so many years. Jamie's nan had died a couple of years ago. Now Jamie only had his granddad. He had not had any contact with any of his dad's family since his dad had left.

Jamie wondered whether Mike cooked dinner for himself every night. Did he ever cry like he had done that day at the funeral?

Mike opened a wooden cupboard and stretched up to the top. He pulled down an old leather scrapbook.

He blew off the dust and ran his hand over the cover a couple of times. For a few seconds, he stared silently at the book. Then he looked at Jamie.

"I want to tell you about a man named Kenny Wilcox," he said.

"I must have been about fifteen and I was playing football outside in my street – just like I did everyday – when a man who was taking his dog out for a walk stopped to watch us play for a while. Not for long. But long enough."

Mike had a distant look in his eye as he told Jamie the story, like he was going back to his childhood as he spoke.

"The man walked his dog around the block but when

he came back he asked if he could speak to me for a second. He told me he was a coach at Hawkstone and asked me if I wanted to come down for a trial the next week."

"Wow! That must have been amazing!" said Jamie, shaking his head. He'd heard lots about Mike's career before but not about how he'd first got spotted. "The greatest day of your life, right? How much did you sign for again?"

"Slow down, JJ – we haven't even got to the trial yet! Anyway, that day was the first day I met Kenny. A great man. The best football coach I ever knew."

"How well did you play in the trial, Mike? You must have nailed it for them to sign you up."

"Just the opposite, actually. My problem in those days was I was big – *too* big for my age, really. I was strong and good in the air, but not too clever on the ground.

"The strikers that I was up against at the trial were the worst type for me, all small and quick. I just couldn't get near them.

"After the trial, I didn't wait to hear who they were offering contracts to. I just left. I was gutted because I knew I hadn't done enough. I suppose that's how you felt the other day, wasn't it, JJ? It feels like you haven't done yourself justice, doesn't it?"

Jamie nodded. Well, at least Mike had shown that it

was possible to bounce back from a disastrous trial. Jamie imagined how good Mike must have been when he was younger. In all the photos he had seen of Mike in the Hawks kit he'd looked so strong. Like a giant that could win any tackle he went in for.

"What do you think would have happened if you hadn't had your injury, Mike? How good were you going to be?" Jamie heard himself ask.

Mike's eyes widened. He hadn't been expecting that question. He took a deep breath and blew the air out of his mouth before he answered.

"Who knows, Jamie? It wasn't meant to be for me. That's what I've always told myself. And, anyway, I'm happy with what I've got."

"Yeah, but you could have been a millionaire instead of a. . ."

Jamie stopped himself. There was nothing wrong with being an electrician and Mike was still working part-time, doing odd jobs around the neighbourhood. He knew it had come out wrong though.

"Anyway," said Mike. "Where was I?"

"You were upset after you played rubbish in the trial – just like me!" said Jamie, relieved to get back to the story.

"*Badly*, yes, I played badly. And when I got home I went straight to my room. I just lay on my bed, beating

34

myself up about how I'd blown my chance. Then my mum, your great nan, came into my bedroom.

"'Do you know a man called Kenny Wilcox?' she asked me. I remember she had a strange smile on her face.

"'Of course I know who Kenny Wilcox is,' I said.

"'Well, he'd like to see you, Mike. He's downstairs.'

"I came down to find Kenny sitting on our couch with a glass of brandy in one hand and a slice of cake in the other. Apparently, he'd knocked on every door in the street to find out where I lived.

"He got up and shook my hand and, when we sat down, he asked me where I'd got to after the trial. Before I could answer, he told me that he thought I had the potential to be a professional footballer."

"For real?" said Jamie. "Even after you'd had a bad game in the trial! He must have seriously rated you."

Mike nodded.

"He said I still had work to do on my game before they could take things further, though. He told me that I had to improve my pace on the turn and that my touch and distribution needed to be better too. He said that he could help me to do that.

"He told me that to help the Youth Team players at Hawkstone, he'd devised a set of exercises to improve every aspect of a footballer's game. He told me to practise the ones specifically designed to develop pace and passing and then come back and see him in a few months. He gave me his book of drills and then he left."

"How long before you went back, then? And what did your mates say when you told them that you were going to sign for Hawkstone?" asked Jamie. "They must have been well jealous!"

"I didn't tell anyone about it. I didn't want to put any more pressure on myself. I just practised and practised – every day. I hardly saw my mates, to be honest. I just kept working on those exercises and thinking about what Kenny had said. Even when I'd had enough, I'd just carry on and carry on. That was how much I wanted it.

"After two months I was so much more quick and nimble on my feet and my first touch had come on a bundle too. I went back to see Kenny and he got me to join in with a Youth Team session straight away. After twenty minutes, he hauled me into his office and I signed schoolboy terms there and then.

"A couple of weeks later, I brought Kenny's book back to him and thanked him for lending it to me. He took it off me, scribbled something in it and then handed it back to me. He told me that at the end of the season the club was restructuring its youth system and that he would be leaving. . . It turned out I was one of the last players that he ever signed.

"So he told me to hold on to it and pass it on to someone else who needed it.

"Football's changed in lots of ways since my day," said Mike. "But pace and skill will always win you matches."

He tapped the old book with his knuckles and put it on Jamie's lap.

"I think Kenny would have approved," he said.

In off the Post

Thursday 3 August

The book smelled precious. Through the smell, Jamie felt he was somehow connecting with all the other boys that had read it in the past.

He wondered if any of Hawkstone's great players had used the book when they were trying to break through.

Every page was crammed with diagrams and drills. They were all immaculately handwritten. All of Kenny's knowledge of the game was here before Jamie, written on these pages. It was as if he had Kenny as his personal coach.

On the inside of the cover there was an inscription. It read:

To Mike,
Success is about desire.
The only limits are the ones you place on
yourself.
Kenny Wilcox

Jamie smiled. He thumbed through the pages, looking at all the different drills. He shook his head as he thought about all the work that must have gone into it. It was too much for him though. He couldn't just lie there in bed and read about the drills; he had to get out on the pitch and *do* them.

Jamie's feet started to tingle. His body was beginning to rev itself up.

He bounced to the floor and did thirty-three press-ups in three sets of eleven. He liked doing sets of eleven because he could think of the Number Eleven shirt while he did each set. He wanted that Kingfield School Number Eleven shirt so badly.

He pushed the air hard out of his mouth each time he lifted himself off the carpet. He made himself angry by thinking about how Dillon Simmonds had wound him up during the trials and how much he wanted to teach him a lesson next term.

He let his chest and arms have all of the angry strength that was meant for Dillon.

After he'd done the last press-up, Jamie stood up and looked at himself in the mirror. He raised his arms up into the air like he'd just won a boxing match. His chest was heaving. He flexed his pecs. They looked good.

So what if some people saw him as a skinny ginger kid? So what if he still didn't have any hair under his arms?

This morning Jamie felt strong. He flexed his biceps and felt his golf ball muscles. Anyone that doubted him didn't know how much strength he had inside him.

Jamie carefully packed the book into his bag and flew down the stairs. He couldn't wait to get down to Sunningdale. Couldn't wait to get started on Kenny's drills.

As he put his hand on the door knob to leave, the post dropped through the letter box. Jamie bent down to pick it up. It wasn't like anyone ever wrote to him, but for some reason he always found the post arriving exciting.

Among the pizza fliers, minicab cards and bills, Jamie immediately noticed a brown envelope poking out menacingly from the middle of the pile. *Kingfield School – Rise to the Challenge* said the red lettering on the postmark.

His school report. This was not good news. He'd

promised his mum that changing schools wouldn't affect his marks, but after the term he'd had, he knew that this report wasn't going to be a cracker.

He had to think quickly.

He decided to take it up to his room and keep it there until he'd worked out how to play things. Maybe he could take the worst pages out. It was his first report from Kingfield so his mum wouldn't know how long it should be. . .

"What have you got there, Jamie?" his mum called as he started up the stairs. "That wouldn't happen to be your report, would it? It's due around now."

Sprung.

"Err . . . I'm not sure . . . yeah . . . I think it might be actually," said Jamie, trying to sound surprised. He wasn't a great actor.

"I was just . . . erm . . . going to sort of have a look in my room . . . see what it said and everything."

"Oh, were you? Well, how about I make a cup of tea and we have a look at it together?"

⑩
The Report

They sat down on either side of the kitchen table and Jamie's mum flicked her finger under the flap of the envelope, opening it without a tear. She pulled out the red booklet.

Jamie flinched. It looked evil.

"Jamie Johnson – 8R," she read out loud.

FRENCH – GRADE D

Overall, this was a disappointing couple of terms for Jamie. After a good start, Jamie's progress tailed off rapidly.

Poor concentration in the classroom has led to poor marks in his homework. I note that Jamie is one of the youngest members of the class and I am therefore hoping that his negative attitude is a case of immaturity rather than anything more serious.

G GILLES

Jamie's mum looked cross.

"I thought you enjoyed French, Jamie?"

"It's boring," replied Jamie. "He just talks in French the whole time."

"I think that's the point."

Jamie's mum shook her head.

MATHS – GRADE D

Jamie has good natural ability with numbers. However, if he thinks this alone will be enough to carry him through the course, he is wrong. As the syllabus becomes increasingly complex, Jamie will find himself in serious danger of being left behind.

In isolation, Jamie can be an engaging and talented pupil but he needs to choose the company he keeps more wisely and start applying himself far better.

J BARNWELL

"What does he mean, Jamie? Who's he talking about?"

"How should I know? I sit next to Tesh – you know him.

There's nothing wrong with Tesh," said Jamie stubbornly.

He didn't mention the fact that he also sat next to Ollie in maths. He knew Barnwell hated Ollie and, although his mum hadn't even met Ollie, she'd already decided he was a bad influence.

"Mr Barnwell's just sad, Mum. He can't control the class, that's all it is."

HISTORY – GRADE E

As a new pupil and one starting in the middle of the school year, one might have expected that Jamie would want to create a good impression. Suffice to say this has not been the case where I am concerned.

Having become disillusioned with Jamie's attitude, I recently asked him what he hoped to achieve with his life. His response – that he wanted to be a professional footballer – said everything about where this young man's head is. The fact of the matter is, Jamie is in the bottom three pupils in his year and seems to have no interest in improving his situation.

B CLAUNT

Jamie's mum looked at him with angry eyes.

"What was the agreement about you joining Kingfield?"

she said, waving the report around as she spoke so that pages fluttered, making a sound like a kite on a windy day.

"Mum, I know. I'll try harder next year. I promise!"

ENGLISH – GRADE C

Regrettably, Jamie seems to think that disrupting his classmates and playing the joker is more important than positive participation in my lessons.

This is all the more frustrating because – in the rarest of flashes – he has shown his true capabilities.

I have set Jamie's class a small project to complete over the summer. I strongly suggest that he hands this in on time and produces a quality of work that more accurately reflects his abilities.

D C GARRICK

PHYSICAL EDUCATION – GRADE B

Although not a particularly experienced rugby or basketball player, Jamie used his speed and hand/eye co-ordination to make an impressive start to his sporting pursuits at Kingfield.

The football trials were clearly a mixed day for Jamie. He needs to work on some elements of his game – not least controlling his temper – but in terms of natural ability there is plainly some potential.

P MARSDEN

"See, Mum, I've got potential! Sport's what matters to me. That's what I'm good at!" said Jamie. He knew he was lucky that Marsden hadn't written anything about the sending-off.

"Football is *not* the be all and end all of everything, Jamie. It's maths and English that are going to get you a job, when this football phase of yours is finished. When are you going to learn that?"

It's not a *phase*, Jamie thought to himself, but he knew his mum would really blow her top if he started arguing with her now. There were more pages to come but she flicked through to the head teacher's report at the end, shaking her head.

THE HEAD TEACHER

Some early warning signs here.

Jamie will be aware that we made allowances in order for him to join the school in the middle of the academic year and he therefore bears a certain amount of responsibility for making this work.

Jamie should worry less about what others think of him and more about what he thinks of himself.

All of us, but mostly Jamie, must ensure that this is a temporary blip rather than the start of a slippery slope.

T PATTEN

Jamie's mum closed the report and shut her eyes. Her body seemed to be shaking.

"You've let me down big time, Jamie. I spent ages getting you into this school and what do you do? You throw it back in my face. I work every day and you give me no help around the house whatsoever. You can't even be bothered to do the shopping for me when I ask you. I've had it with you.

"All you're interested in is football. Meanwhile, your education is going down the pan and you couldn't care less. Are you planning to actually achieve anything with your life, Jamie?"

"Yes I am. I'm going to be a professional f—"

"Don't! Don't you dare say that! Until you do that English project and start pulling your weight around the house, you're not going to kick another ball. Do you understand me?"

Panic and rage rushed through Jamie. It was the summer holidays! How could she?

"What? No way! You can't do that! You've got no right to tell me what I can and can't do. That's illegal."

Jamie stood up violently, pushing away the table. His mum's mug of tea tipped over, spilling its contents across the report. But she didn't make a move to clear it up.

"You don't understand," said Jamie, desperately trying to keep his calm. "I'm just getting somewhere with my football. Mike's given me this amazing book . . . please. . ."

"This is not a discussion, Jamie. No football until you pull your finger out," Jamie's mum responded. All the emotion had gone from her voice. "And you can clean up this mess for a start."

Then she walked out of the room. Jamie had never seen his mum like that before.

But she wasn't the only one who was angry.

11

Broken Dreams

Wednesday 9 August

For the next week, Jamie did not say a word to his mum. Breakfasts came and went in silence. He ate dinners in his room.

She'd organized all her shifts at the hospital to be late-night ones so that she could keep an eye on him during the day. He couldn't believe she was behaving like this. What had he ever done to her?

The only good thing was that Jamie had an escape route. He'd worked out what time his mum had her break during the night shift. That meant that, if he wanted, he could wait and make sure he was there when she made her call home to check up on him and then get his bike out and go down and meet Ollie, Tesh and the others at the bus shelter.

The rest of the time he was in his room playing football games on his computer, listening to music or looking through Kenny Wilcox's book. All he thought about was the day he could get out there and play again.

He didn't want to be anywhere near his mum. How could she do this to him? How could she pretend she cared about him and then stop him from doing the most important thing in his life?

Anyway, she couldn't force him to do his English project or anything else.

If she wanted a battle, she could have one. He'd make her pay.

One afternoon, locked away in his room, Jamie thought about how he could punish his mum for the way she was treating him.

He could never talk to her again. Then she would be sorry.

He could run away. Live with Mike. Or try to find his dad. He had to be out there somewhere. That would make her sorry for what she'd done. Jamie imagined his mum going into his room and finding the window open and Jamie gone. She'd look in the wardrobe and find all his best clothes gone. And his boots.

He wouldn't be there any more and it would all be her fault. She would collapse on to the bed crying, beating her fists into the mattress just like she had when Jamie's dad had left. That was six years ago but Jamie could still remember it like it had just happened. He could remember how seeing his mum cry had made him feel more upset than anything else in the world.

Even thinking about it now made him feel sad again.

Jamie thought about how much his mum would miss him if he ran away. How she would always miss him, every second of every day.

And the more he thought about it, the less angry he became with his mum and the more he began to feel sorry for her.

She hadn't talked about Jamie's dad for years. Did she still love him, even though he left her? Did she want to find a new husband? Did she even have time for a boyfriend? The only man she ever seemed to talk to these days was that guy from the hospital who gave her lifts to work. What was his name? Geoffrey? Jeremy?

He knew the reason his mum had to work the whole time was to pay the bills and that when she came home she had to start on the housework and the cooking. All this for Jamie.

The only things she asked for in return were for Jamie to be nice to her and to try to do well at school.

And what had Jamie done? He'd let her down on both counts.

And now he was ignoring her because she'd asked him to do some English homework for the school he'd begged her to let him join.

Jamie's heart started to feel heavy. There was a painful lump inside his throat. He felt embarrassed. He was lucky to have his mum. He wanted to go downstairs and hug her and say he was sorry.

He wanted her to be proud of him like she used to be.

Jamie blinked away a tear. He sat down at his desk and turned on the lamp. He could feel the glow of the bulb against his cheek as he stared at the empty white pages of his workbook. How was he going to fill them?

He tried to remember what Mr Garrick had asked them to do for homework.

"A story," he'd said. "A story of triumph over adversity, of winning against the odds. . ."

Jamie pulled the lid from his pen and began writing. He knew the story he wanted to tell.

Mike Johnson – Broken Dreams

Jamie took great care to style each letter as neatly as possible, before grasping his ruler and underlining the title perfectly.

Then the strangest thing happened: once he started writing, he couldn't stop.

Normally when he did his homework – *if* he did his homework – each sentence would take for ever. But somehow, tonight, whole paragraphs were spilling out of his brain and on to the paper in front of him. Because he was writing about football, it seemed easy.

As he recalled the story of Mike being spotted playing in the street and being invited to go for a trial, Jamie's thoughts instantly became words on the page. For once, it didn't seem difficult or boring; he just remembered and wrote.

After an hour of furious writing, Jamie put down his pen to give his aching hand a rest. He flicked back over the pages. He had written so much. Now he just had to do the ending:

Mike Johnson walked out of the hospital and he knew that his Hawkstone career was over before it had even begun.

So in the end, Mike Johnson never became a Hawks hero. He never became a millionaire either. He was luckier than that. He became a happy man.

After he'd finished his story, Jamie went downstairs to show it to his mum.

She was watching TV. Jamie crept up behind her. He

wanted it to be a surprise.

"I don't want you to hate me, Mum," he said, giving her his story to read.

"Hate you?" his mum said, turning off the TV to look at Jamie. "How could I hate you? You're the most precious thing in my life. That's why I want the best for you."

"I know," Jamie said.

(12) Back in the Game

Thursday 10 August

Jamie's mum had really liked his story about her dad. She'd said it was vivid and she was sure it would get a good mark, even if it was about football.

And they had agreed that if his school work improved next term, then Jamie playing football was OK. Best of all was that Jamie's mum had lifted the ban during the holidays as "an act of good faith".

Now Jamie was back!

The next day he burst into Sunningdale at his very top speed. He had so much energy to burn after being locked in his room for so long. All that time thinking had only made him more determined to do everything he could to earn a spot in the A's.

Jamie ran towards a pitch right on the far side of the park. He sprinted straight past the First Team boys who were in the middle of their daily training session. He didn't have any more time to watch what they were up to and he didn't care what they thought of him. There were only three weeks of the holidays left. He had to concentrate on himself.

Jamie sat down on a bench and got out Kenny's book. In his room, he'd found a whole section on wingers. It was the perfect training programme for him.

Here's what it said:

Wing Play
Two of the fundamentals in wing play are pace and dribbling.

Jamie nodded his head and carried on reading.

First, we'll deal with pace, which is one of the biggest trump cards any winger can possess.

The most precious pace in football is over five yards. Defenders may be quicker than you over longer distances but, if you can knock the ball past them and get in a cross or a shot, as a winger you have done your job.

The following drill, if repeated consistently with all your effort, will increase your pace over the first five yards. And remember, your pace is not only for attacking. When your team doesn't have the ball, you need to pull in track your man and help win the ball back.

Jamie knew he had natural pace. All his old sprint medals from The Grove were evidence of that. But he also knew that to get into the A's he had to get even quicker. His eyes scanned the drill.

The Drill
1. Start by performing small bouncing movements on the spot.
2. Turn to the left, sprint, and touch a line five yards away with your left foot.
3. Turn back to the right, sprint ten yards, and touch the far line with your right foot.
4. Turn back to the left, sprint five yards to the start line to finish.
5. During the recovery period dribble with the ball back and forth across the drill (three

times) before leaving the ball at the opposite side and returning to the start. Never forget the ball - that is what this is all about.

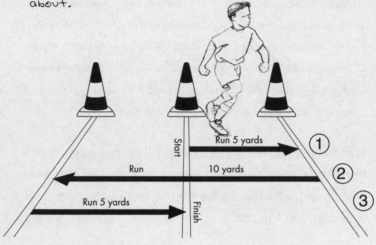

Jamie put down his tracksuit and his bag as markers. As he bounced on the spot, he pulled the summer scents into his lungs. The grass had just been cut and it made the air smell fresh and clean. Jamie was ready to roll.

He took one final, deep breath. Then he rocketed forward towards his first marker with an electric burst of pace.

He imagined himself burning past a defender to get to the by-line and pull a cross back. He pumped his arms hard as he ran to find his extra, "turbo" gear.

He threw himself into it. Having missed out on training for the whole of the last week, today he wanted to go to the very limit of his body's capabilities.

Even when he thought he had nothing else left to give, he kept pushing himself that little bit further. In the end, he did the drill eleven times.

The sweat streamed down his body as his legs galloped across the grass.

Jamie was taking a leap in a new direction.

⑬ Next Step

Monday 21 August

Jamie practised the speed drills over and over again. To make it harder for himself, sometimes he changed things so he started facing the wrong way or lying down.

He used his stopwatch and noted down his time after every set. Each day, he made sure he didn't leave Sunningdale until he'd recorded a new personal best. Although he really wanted to move on to the other drills, Jamie carried on doing the speed drills until he'd taken two and a half seconds off the time he'd started the week with.

But after ten days of solid speed work, Jamie wanted more. He wanted to take the next step.

According to the book, that was dribbling.

This is what Kenny's book said:

Dribbling

With football's increasing emphasis on strength and fitness, the ability to beat a player with skill is a priceless commodity.

If you have that ability, cherish it and nurture it because you may well be the difference between your team winning and losing a game.

When you are dribbling, remember to:
- Run straight at your opponent. Your positive, direct play will put you on the front foot and unnerve the defender.
- Try your tricks in the attacking third of the pitch. Beating your man on the halfway line is nice but not dangerous. Beating your man in the penalty area is lethal!

There was one trick that Jamie really wanted to perfect, because although it was simple, it could make even the best defender look like a fool. The book explained it brilliantly:

Beating your opponent on the outside

You don't have to do step-overs and back-heels to beat a defender. Balance and change of direction, allied to pace, are your most dangerous weapons.

One of the most effective ways to beat a defender is to run at them at full pace and, when they are just outside of tackling distance, to take a small touch to make it look as though you are going to go on the inside.

The defender moves to cover the inside channel but if the attacker then quickly knocks the ball back down the outside of the defender and, at the same time, injects a decisive change of pace, the defender is wrong-footed and helpless to stop the attacker.

This is how it looks in a one-on-one situation:

Inject extra pace for change of direction

It's a good trick to have up your sleeve and the following drill is a good way to practise it.

Find a wall and lay your markers down near that wall in a bendy line, as shown. Have some of the markers close to each other and some a bit further away. To start the drill kick the ball to yourself off the wall. However the ball comes back to you - left or right, high or low - that is the start of your dribble. The fact that it's unpredictable is good. That's the way it will be in matches.

So control the ball with one touch as it comes to you off the wall and then dribble through your markers as quickly as you can, using both the inside and outside of your boot as you go. Dribble up and down the line of markers three times and then take a break. You can practise juggling the ball while you warm down and prepare for your next set.

Bollards

Bounce ball off wall to start

Wall

If you can master the dribble, your defender will have a tough time stopping you in a game.

Jamie looked around. He was in the middle of the park. There were no walls that he could use. But there was an old hut by the side of the pitch. Jamie realized he could use the back of the hut as his wall. He immediately started working on the drill.

He practised dribbling through the markers over and over again. He wanted to become the best dribbler in the whole school. He visualized himself sprinting at Dillon and Dillon falling over as Jamie jinked past him.

After five days, Jamie started adding his own bits to the exercise. First he tried hitting the ball harder on to the wall of the hut at the start so that it would really test his control when it came to him. Then he began to force himself to look up at the markers in front of him when he was dribbling, rather than looking down at the ball at his feet. He wanted to feel the ball with his feet, not look for it with his eyes. He wanted his body to memorize these changes of direction so that they became an instinct for him. He didn't want to have to think about it during a game. He just wanted to do it.

Jamie's feet were learning a new way to play.

(14)

Final Test

Sunday 3rd September –
Last Day of the Holidays

The days and the drills flew by. Jamie couldn't believe it when the last day of the holidays came around. He'd spent every single day down at the park. He'd had a few texts and missed calls from Ollie and Tesh to see if he wanted to go down to the shopping centre but Jamie had never found the time. His mind was so completely filled with Kenny's book and working on his game. When Ollie and Tesh saw him play next term, then they would realize what he'd been up to all holidays.

Jamie decided to do an extra long session to end the holidays with. It was his final chance to prepare himself before the start of term. He'd had a look at some of the free-kick exercises in the book and he wanted to finish with those. If he could start the season by bending a set-piece right into the top corner, Marsden would have to sit up and take notice.

Jamie was all set up and just about to start when, out of the corner of his eye, he noticed one of the First Eleven boys jogging towards him from the pitches on the other side of the park.

It was Danny Miller! He even looked like a professional player just in the way he jogged. It was hard to believe he was only sixteen.

But what did Danny want with him?

Jamie was nervous. He didn't quite know how to position himself as Danny got nearer and nearer. In the end he just stood there with his foot on the ball and his hands on his hips.

"All right, mate," said Danny, wiping a bead of sweat from his forehead. It was hot.

"All right," Jamie replied.

"Listen, we've got a little game going on, but one of our players has just pulled his hammy. Do you fancy making up the numbers?"

"Seriously?" asked Jamie. He didn't want them to get him over there just to laugh at him again like they had when they'd seen him commentating to himself the other week.

"Listen, if you don't fancy it, mate. . ."

"No – it's all right, I'm in. Let me just get my stuff together."

Jamie was trying to act cool but underneath he was so excited. He was going to train with the Firsts!

He and Danny jogged towards the other pitch, exchanging passes on the way.

"You're at Kingfield, aren't you?" asked Danny.

"Yeah, I'm just about to go into Year Nine."

"Yeah – I thought I recognized you. What position do you play? Oh, my name's Danny by the way."

As if Jamie didn't know who he was!

"Everyone, this is Jamie," said Danny, as they jogged on to the pitch. "He's going to play with us today. He's a left-winger."

Jamie looked at the First Eleven as they each sized him up. He tried to force a smile but he was nervous about what they were all thinking about him.

"Hey, it's Mini Miller!" said one of the bigger lads, who was on the team playing in skins. "Right, he's ours then."

The boy beckoned Jamie over to his team.

He seemed to be the captain of the team in skins and Danny the captain of the other. That meant Jamie was going to have to play against Danny Miller.

Jamie nodded and took off his top. His white, hairless, bony chest stood out among the muscle-bound six-packs around him. He hated playing in skins.

And then, without any more warning or Jamie even having a chance to introduce himself to his teammates, they started.

Jamie couldn't believe what he was doing. He was actually training with the First Eleven! He was in awe of them. They were all about twice his size. And they all had stubble.

They were men and Jamie was a boy.

The pace was amazing. They were playing one-touch passes, making runs off the ball, clattering into tackles and shouting orders to each other. They seemed to know each other's games inside out.

Jamie's excitement quickly divided itself into fear and nerves. He knew that when the ball came to him, he wouldn't have a clue what to do with it. The last thing he wanted to do was try something flashy and make a fool of himself again.

Not that Jamie's team had much of the ball anyway. They had to get it off Danny first. While everyone else was rushing, tackling and sprinting, Danny seemed to be playing the game in cruise control. Although half of Jamie's team were trying to tackle him, somehow he seemed able to brush them off and turn away from trouble without even trying.

No wonder a few of the professional clubs had tried to sign Danny already. He'd said that he wanted to finish school first though.

It seemed like ages before Jamie's team got good possession of the ball. But as soon as they did, they spread it out to the wing, where Jamie was standing, waiting.

"Yes, Jamie! Lay it back," one of the players on his team shouted at him. The ball was coming towards Jamie and they wanted a quick pass.

Jamie knew he should pass it first time, like they all were, but he wanted a touch first to make sure he had it under control.

He should have moved towards the ball too, but he waited for it to come to him. It was too late.

Jamie hadn't even got control of the ball before a defender flew straight through the back of him. He took Jamie's legs away completely, leaving him in a heap on the ground.

Now Jamie knew what it felt like to be taken out by a First Eleven player. It wasn't a nice feeling.

"Hey, Quincy!" shouted one of the boys on Jamie's side. "Go easy, mate, he's only a kid."

As if to show there were no hard feelings, Quincy Oromuyi offered Jamie his hand to help him up. But as he did so, he said in a low voice, "Not so easy against *real* defenders, is it?"

Jamie let go of Quincy's hand immediately. He realized now that Quincy was the one who'd been laughing the most that other week when they had seen him commentating on himself.

Jamie knew he had it in for him.

But what could he do? The guy was a giant, way stronger than him.

Quincy could foul him all he wanted and there was not a thing Jamie could do about it. It made him angry.

When play restarted, Danny continued to control the game. He was dribbling the ball around the players on Jamie's team and, every time he beat a man, Quincy was clapping his hands, shouting "Olé!"

Jamie looked at Quincy and felt a river of frustrated energy start to rush through his veins.

A thought pushed its way into Jamie's head: you might not be able to have a go at Quincy but you can go and win the ball. Now go and do it! He was shouting at himself inside his own brain.

Danny Miller still had the ball. He was on the edge of the box.

Pounding his legs on the turf, Jamie reached top speed straight away, catching up with Danny just as he was pulling his right foot back to unleash a shot.

Jamie launched himself forward and got in a crunching tackle, blocking the ball just as Danny made contact.

There was a loud bang as Jamie parried all the power that Danny had put into the intended shot.

The ball squirmed away, sorry to have been involved in such a hefty collision.

Both Danny and Jamie tumbled to the ground, with Jamie's momentum spinning him over a couple of times when he hit the deck.

He was still feeling dizzy, when he suddenly felt a sharp pain on his head.

"Oi!" shouted Quincy, who'd grabbed Jamie's hair. "That was a dirty tackle."

"Get off!" shouted Jamie, digging his nails into Quincy's wrist to get him to let go. "I was going for the ball!"

"Watch your temper, little boy," said Quincy. His voice sounded calm but, as he was speaking he was grabbing Jamie's shoulder so hard in a pressure point that it hurt like hell.

"Trust me," Quincy said, menacingly. "You don't want to make me angry."

"Just leave me alone," said Jamie, getting himself free of Quincy's hold. He could feel that he might start crying. That would be the worst possible thing he could do.

He turned away and started walking.

He heard a few of the players on his team shouting his name but he didn't care.

They'd had their fun with him. They'd just got him to play with them so that they could laugh at him again. Why had he even said yes?

He'd had such a good few weeks and got his confidence right back. Now they had ruined everything again for him just as he was about to go back to school.

Jamie shook his head and kicked a pile of grass cuttings as he walked. Why couldn't they have just left him alone?

(15)
Come Back

Jamie slung his bag over his shoulder and headed for the park gates. At least Jack was finally coming home tonight. She'd get him back in the right frame of mind for school.

Jamie suddenly felt a tug on his bag.

"Is that it then, Jamie?"

It was Danny. He'd come after him.

"Yes, that's it. I'm going home."

"Ah come on, Jamie. We've only just started. Your team needs you."

"What – so Quincy can have another go at me? I don't think so."

"Oh, Quincy's OK. He's just like that sometimes. Sees everything as a contest. He likes to test people out, see what they're made of, you know? So you've got to come back and show him."

"Sorry if I fouled you, by the way," said Jamie, sheepishly looking at Danny's strip, which was now covered in dirt. He had gone in a bit hard.

"What are you talking about? It wasn't a foul. It was a great tackle. You're stronger than you look, by the way."

Finally, Jamie cracked a smile.

Jamie came back on to the pitch with just one thing in his mind. He wanted to have a run at Quincy. Yes he was bigger than Jamie. And yes he was stronger than Jamie. But how *good* was he?

As soon as Jamie got the ball, he was determined to find out.

"Turn!" one of the players shouted to Jamie as they laid the ball up the line to him.

Suddenly Jamie's feet took over. His left foot met the ball with a soft, secure touch, flicking it behind his right foot as he twisted himself a hundred and eighty degrees to face the opposition goal.

His feet were strong, springy and fast and they were driving straight towards Quincy. The more Quincy backed away, the more Jamie turned on his turbo gear.

As he approached Quincy, Jamie feigned to go on the

inside before clipping the ball down the outside and changing his pace to dash past him.

Quincy was beaten. He threw out an arm to try and grab Jamie, but it was too late. Jamie was already heading for the by-line.

When he got there, Jamie wedged his boot right under the ball and clipped it up to the far post. It was a beautiful, hanging cross and went right to where one of his teammates was waiting, ready to head the ball down into the net.

Jamie's team were 1 – 0 up. Now Quincy knew what Jamie Johnson was all about.

16
End of the Beginning

The game finished 1 – 1. Danny Miller had curled in an equalizer from the edge of the area to level it up late on.

After training he'd thanked his teammates for giving up so much of their holidays to train everyday and said that it was good to end with a "diplomatic draw".

Jamie was really proud of himself. He knew he'd made his mark. Not only had he set up his team's goal, but when they had been defending, he'd dug in and tracked back. He'd even popped up once in the right-back position!

After the game, most of the First Eleven boys were sitting on the ground with their girlfriends who had come along to meet them. They were all well fit.

Jamie instantly felt his age again. He didn't want to look any of the girls in the eye. He heard one of them say: "Ahh – isn't he cute?" But that just made him more embarrassed. He hated it when girls called him cute.

He got his stuff together and made his way out of the park. He was knackered.

He'd run himself into the ground. But it was worth it. The skills he'd learned from the book were already starting to pay off – and he'd only played one game!

He couldn't wait to tell Mike that he'd trained with the Firsts. And Jack. She'd be back now. But it was already 7.30. By the time he'd got home and had a soak in the bath, it would be nine o'clock before he got round there. Although they'd agreed to meet up tonight, his mum wouldn't be too happy if he had a late one the night before school started. He could tell her everything on the way to school tomorrow, anyway.

"Thanks for playing, Jamie," Danny shouted from the middle of the group of his teammates and their girlfriends. They were all lying on the grass. It was a warm evening.

"Oh, no probs. Thanks for asking," said Jamie, turning around.

Then Danny gave his girlfriend a kiss on the cheek and walked over to Jamie.

"Listen, we'll be training here on Sundays, and Monday

and Friday nights after school for the next few weeks. Do you want to come along? It's always good to have more left-footers."

Jamie was in shock. He couldn't believe it. The Firsts wanted *him* to train with *them* all the time!

"Err. . . Yeah! That'd be great. Thanks," he said.

"Nice one," said Danny. "See you tomorrow night, then. Six o'clock."

That night, after a long bath, Jamie sank back into his pillow and pulled the duvet right up under his chin.

His legs ached. But in a good way. They had given everything these holidays.

He knew that next term wasn't going to be easy.

First of all, he had to keep his marks up, otherwise he wouldn't even be allowed to play football.

Then there was Dillon, who would be in his face from day one.

And, worse still, Jamie was sure he would be in the dreaded B Team for the first games of the new season.

He just knew it. How could Marsden put him in the A's after what had happened at the trials?

But the funny thing was Jamie didn't feel worried.

He felt ready.

Part
TWO

Back to School

Monday 4 September –
First Day Back

Normally, Jamie met Jack at 8.30 a.m. at the lamp post between their houses for the walk to school but today he'd already been standing outside for about ten minutes and there was still no sign of her.

He turned his phone on to check the time. It was 8.42. There wasn't even time to knock on her door and see if she'd overslept. Jamie knew he had to get going otherwise he'd be late for the first day back.

He started to jog up the road but then he felt something vibrate inside his trouser pocket. It was his phone. A text had come through. Jamie read it as he ran.

It was from Jack: Hey! Got back early! When r u coming round?

It had been sent at 5.31 p.m. yesterday. Jamie must have been training down at Sunningdale when she'd sent it and what with having his bath and getting everything ready for school before he went to sleep, he hadn't had a chance to check his messages last night.

He felt bad. Jack must have thought that he'd forgotten their arrangement or, even worse, that he was ignoring her for some reason. As if! He couldn't wait to tell her everything.

Jack would be cool though. Once he'd told her that he was now training with the First Eleven, that would be all she'd want to hear about.

Jamie ended up having to sprint practically the whole way to school just to get there in time. Still, the more fitness training the better. But when he walked into the assembly hall, Jamie had a big shock. He saw that Jack was already sitting down and next to her, in the seat that Jamie always sat, was Nicki Forbes. She had taken Jamie's place!

Nicki and Jamie didn't get on at all. Nicki had been Jack's best friend at Kingfield before Jamie had joined so she'd always had an attitude with him, like he'd stolen Jack away from her or something.

Jamie knew Nicki would be loving the fact that she

was sitting in his place. It annoyed him to see them talking and laughing together. Jack must have given up Jamie's seat on purpose, to get back at him for not going round yesterday.

Jamie had so much to tell her. There was Kenny Wilcox's book – she could share it, there was some wicked advice for keepers – plus the little matter of the fact that he was now friendly with Danny Miller!

Jamie went straight up to her after assembly. She'd snap out of it once he'd explained.

"Have you got a sec, Jack?" he said, completely ignoring Nicki, who was standing there too.

"I suppose so," said Jack.

"I'll see you for lunch later then, Jack. Yeah?" said Nicki, talking to Jack but giving Jamie an evil look as she spoke.

"Yeah, see you later, Nicks." Jack smiled.

They could talk properly now Nicki was out of the way. Jamie suddenly had an urge to give Jack a massive hug. He hadn't seen her for weeks. But they didn't normally do that, and certainly not in school.

"So how have you been, mate? How was Antigua?" he asked with a lively grin.

Jack's face had turned cold and expressionless as soon as Nicki had gone but Jamie carried on anyway.

"Sorry about last night, by the way. I was down at

Sunningdale till late and my mum's been giving me no end of grief. . . Anyway, I've got so much to tell you. Guess what's happening tonight?"

For a second, Jack's face brightened.

"What are we doing?" she asked.

"No, not us – me. I'm training with the First Eleven down at Sunningdale tonight. They invited me yesterday. You should come down and watch, then we can catch up afterwards."

Jack's face dropped again. She pursed her lips together really tight.

"I can't," she said. "I'm busy. You have a good time."

And then she walked off.

Jamie felt a bit weird. He thought Jack would be happy for him but she was being really strange. Maybe she was jealous – she probably wanted to train with the Firsts herself. She was still really angry about not being able to play in the boys' team.

But if Jack had a problem with Jamie training with the Firsts, that was her problem, not his.

Jamie had to push Jack to the back of his mind. Besides, there were plenty of other things to think about. Like the fact that the first games of the season were tomorrow and the teams were being announced at break.

(18)

Make or
Break-time

As soon as the bell went, Jamie headed straight for the sports hall. Despite the fact that, deep down, he was sure he'd be in the B team, he still had jolts of electricity running through him.

Maybe, just maybe, Marsden would take a chance and stick him in the A's. After all, he had said that Jamie had "potential" in his report.

But before Jamie could even get to see the teams he had to get his way past another obstacle.

Dillon Simmonds had already got there first. Jamie could have done with having Jack on his side for this one. She was so much cleverer than Dillon that she could usually put him in his place with one sentence. But Jamie was going to have to go it alone this time.

Dillon was leaning against the noticeboard, casting his eyes over the teams. As soon as he saw Jamie coming, he started tutting and shaking his head.

"Ah, still not managed to grow over the holidays then, Johnson?" he said in mock sympathy. "Don't worry, your voice might break one day . . . but you'll still be a little ginger minger."

Dillon was laughing really loudly at his own pathetic joke.

"Good to see you too, Dillon," said Jamie, preparing to deliver the line he'd practised in the mirror during the holidays. "Listen, if you haven't got enough cash to buy some Clearasil, I don't mind lending you a couple of quid."

"Come to see what team you're in tomorrow, have you?" said Dillon, ignoring Jamie's response. "Let's have a look, shall we?"

Dillon turned to the noticeboard and dragged his fat, grubby finger through the list of names in the A team to face St Antony's tomorrow. "Not here, are you?" he hissed. "What a surprise that is, after your brilliant penalty in the trials."

He was enjoying every moment of the pain he was putting Jamie through.

"Which means you must be here, in the B's. . . Ah, yes, here you are in the lame old B's, the team that no one cares about. Exactly where you deserve to be. Oh, and who's captain of the A's? Oh yeah, that's right – it's me.

"Good luck," Dillon said with a fake smile as he pushed Jamie out of the way. Then he walked off, taking his stinking, disgusting body with him.

It hadn't exactly been a great first day back for Jamie. Not only had he had to deal with Dillon's disses and the fact that he'd been put in the B's, but he seemed to have managed to fall out with his best friend too.

At lunch, Jack had sat with Nicki and completely ignored him. He'd sat with Ollie and Tesh instead. Even though Jack was only on the next table, it felt like she was miles away.

It was just as well, then, Jamie thought as he walked out through the school gates, that he had something really special to look forward to this evening.

19
Top Tip

After school, Jamie had popped home to get changed and have another quick flick through Kenny Wilcox's book. Before he left, he even slipped in twenty minutes of French vocab to keep his mum sweet.

Then he sprinted straight down to Sunningdale. He didn't want to be late. Danny had said 6 p.m. Jamie was there for 5.50.

Just knowing that Danny and the rest of the First Eleven squad wanted Jamie to train with them gave him such a massive lift. The frustrations of the day seemed to fly away.

For Jamie, having a ball at his feet made him feel the same way his mum must when she had a big mug of tea in her hands. It relaxed him. Made him feel comfortable.

When the others arrived and they picked the teams, Jamie was one of the first people that Danny picked to be on his side. He brimmed with pride as he took his place behind Danny, waiting to see who else they were going to have on their team.

By the time the game started, Jamie felt super confident. He made sure that he never rushed himself in possession, always taking time to pick out the right pass. He played a couple of one-twos with Danny that completely split open the opposition defence.

Whenever he had the opportunity, he skipped down the line. He even hit the post when he cut inside and hit a shot with his right foot. He struck it so sweetly he almost didn't feel it.

They finished the session by playing the Crossbar Challenge, to see who could hit the crossbar first from the edge of the area. Jamie and Danny were the only ones who hit the bar with their first attempts.

"You looking forward to the matches tomorrow, then, Jamie?" said Danny as they sat down behind the goal watching the others trying to hit the bar. Danny was undoing his sweaty shin pads from the back of his heavily muscled calves.

"Yeah – I'm well up for it," said Jamie. "I can't wait to play in a proper competitive game for Kingfield. I only joined in January."

"Oh, right," said Danny. "So you're in with Dillon Simmonds and that lot, are you?"

"Yup." Jamie tried to keep the grimace from his face when that ugly name was mentioned.

"Sounds like a pretty good team, with him at the back and you in attack. Bet Marsden's happy with his lot this year?"

Jamie gritted his teeth, drawing the air in through the sides of his mouth. He was going to have to tell Danny that he was in the B's. It was so embarrassing. Danny probably wouldn't want him to train with the Firsts any more when he found out. But there was no point in Jamie lying. Danny would find out soon enough.

"Yeah . . . well, that's not the team for tomorrow, anyway. I'm . . . sort of . . . in the B's," Jamie said. He felt like he'd let Danny down in some way. "I had an absolute nightmare in the trials."

"Oh, OK," said Danny. "Well, you'll just have to turn it on tomorrow then, won't you? Just do your thing. Marsden's a good coach. He knows how to spot a player."

The branches of the tall oak trees rustled above Jamie's head. It was 7:45 in the evening and the sun was starting its descent.

The others had left half an hour ago, but Jamie had

stayed on to do some more dribbling drills. He'd been using the hut as his wall again, really hammering the ball at it to test his reflexes when it rebounded to him.

Now he was juggling the ball as he walked. He wanted to see if he could keep it up the whole way to the gates of the park without letting it drop. It was another drill in itself.

But a sudden stirring noise behind Jamie made him lose control of the ball. He turned around to see what the noise was, allowing the ball to bounce away from him.

That was when Jamie saw him. There was a man sitting in the hut. The same hut he'd been using for his dribbling exercise. He must have been there the whole time.

The hut smelled like the men's toilets at the Hawks stadium and there were always old bottles strewn around the ground next to it, but there was never anyone there. Until today.

The man sitting in the hut looked weird. His skin was brown, but not brown like he'd just come back from holiday. It was a deeper kind of colour, dirtier. His hair was a mixture of black and grey. It was long and greasy.

He had a beard, too, which was growing at different lengths and glistened in places as if a snail had crawled across it.

Lying on the floor next to the man was a panting dog.

Its grey and black coat was the same colour as the man's beard. It seemed more like a wolf than a dog. There was something really strange about its eyes too. One of them was brown but the other was a bright shade of blue. It looked as if it had a glass eye.

The man had his legs up on the bench and a bottle sticking out from his worn jacket. His hands were covered in mud and grime.

Both he and the dog were glaring at Jamie. Were they angry that Jamie had been using the hut to practise with? If so, why hadn't the man said something?

The ball had come to rest by the side of the hut but Jamie didn't want to get it. He stood there motionless, feeling the man's stare fixed on him. Jamie was scared.

Then the man made a loud snorting noise like a pig and suddenly produced a big load of phlegm that he spat out of his mouth.

Its gloopy green mass landed on the ground right next to Jamie.

He didn't know whether or not the man had meant it; he only knew it was one of the roughest things he'd ever seen.

Like the man's spitting was a starter's gun, the dog immediately got up and ran over to Jamie's ball. It sniffed the ball a few times and bit it. Then it rolled the ball back towards Jamie with its nose.

The ball was covered with the dog's spit but Jamie picked it up anyway. He just wanted to get out of there as soon as possible. He didn't want to run away because that would show he was scared, but he walked as quickly as he could until he was out of the park and into the street. Only then did he turn to look behind him.

But by that time, both the man and the dog had gone.

After that day, Jamie never saw them in the park again. For some reason though, he couldn't shake the image of the man from his mind.

And the strangest thing of all was that even though he couldn't explain it, Jamie had this feeling that, someday, they would meet again.

⑳ Match of the Day

Tuesday 5 September – Match Day

Looking at the clock above the whiteboard, Jamie couldn't believe that it was only 10.20 a.m.

He already felt like he'd been at school for ages, and there were still three hours to go until kick-off. He didn't care any more that he was playing for the B's. He could have been playing for the F's. He just wanted to get out there.

For long periods of this double maths lesson, Jamie had found himself staring out of the window towards the football pitches.

He tried to concentrate on the equations but the only thing in the classroom that was really capturing Jamie's attention was Ollie.

Ollie always went for Mr Barnwell and today he was really going for it – making up for all the lost time over the holidays.

"Right, carry on with your exercises," said Barnwell, sitting at his desk. "Raise your hand if you have a question."

After a couple of minutes of quiet, Ollie looked at Jamie and Tesh. He winked and nodded his head. He clearly had something up his sleeve. Then they realized what it was. He'd just done the most disgusting fart. It was seriously potent.

Then Ollie raised his hand.

"Yes, what is it, Walsh?"

"Sir, could you please come over here for a second? I'm not sure I understand," he said, keeping a completely straight face.

"Very well," said Barnwell, pleasantly surprised at Ollie showing such interest. He got up and practically skipped over to Ollie's desk.

As he stood next to Ollie, his big nose started to twitch as it picked up the scent. Then his eyebrows curled, questioningly.

He'd picked up the smell, all right.

Ollie let him stand there smelling it for a good few seconds before he said: "Um . . . it's OK, sir. I think I've got it now. Thanks anyway, sir."

Barnwell's face went bright red but he didn't do anything. What could he do? He couldn't exactly send Ollie out for that. And anyway, Ollie could just deny it. Where was the proof?

Jamie smiled and let his eyes wander over to the football pitches outside.

In a couple of hours he would be out there playing on them. He imagined himself beating a defender and bending one right into the top corner.

He'd been waiting a long time for this day.

㉑
A Time
for Skill

Jamie took a deep breath. He tapped his chest firmly with the palm of his hand and entered the B team changing room.

A beam of light penetrated the dusky atmosphere, illuminating the tiny particles of dust that were in the air.

Jamie scanned the room for a spare peg and sat down.

Having got changed into his kit, he put on his boots with the utmost care. He'd learned his lesson from the trials; this time, they had to be perfect.

His feet had to be snug at the toe end of the boot to allow him to feel the ball as much as possible, while at the top end, around the tongue, he left it a little looser so he had enough flexibility to curl and dip his shots.

The clacking of the studs said that the team was ready. It was show-time. "C'mon!" Jamie found himself shouting. He wouldn't normally have acted like this – like a captain – before a game but he knew he was one of the best players in the team today so it was up to him to take some responsibility.

"We know we can do this," he told his teammates. "So let's go do it!"

"Come on!" the Kingfield boys roared as they exited the changing room. Tesh and Jamie pushed each other out towards the pitches. They had so much energy.

The adrenalin was pumping through Jamie's veins. And confidence, too. If he could mix it with Danny Miller and that lot, there was no way he should fear the St Antony's B's.

Jamie took a couple of warm-up shots to get his eye in. They flew into the net. Then he did one of the sprint warm-up routines from Kenny Wilcox's book.

He felt powerful. He felt light. He felt dangerous.

UNDER 14s B TEAM MATCH
KINGFIELD   V   ST ANTHONY'S

Mr Marsden was watching the A's game, so the B's had Mr Hitchcock, who was also going to referee. Jamie didn't know him that well – he taught geography to the other set – but he'd heard that he was quite strict. He'd used to be a policeman before he became a teacher.

Mr Hitchcock pushed his glasses up to the bridge of his nose and blew his whistle. They were off.

Right from the start, Kingfield immediately got on top. And soon Jamie got his first chance to have a run at the St Antony's right-back.

Jamie controlled the ball and stopped it dead. He stood upright for a second and looked at his opponent, who had come to close him down.

Then Jamie did the cheekiest thing. He knocked the ball straight through the right-back's legs and ran past him.

Now it was just a test of pace over the first five yards.

No one was going to catch Jamie over five yards. He scorched down the wing. He could hear the defender grunting like an animal in pain as he tried to keep up.

Jamie didn't need to look up. In Alex Marcusfield, the B's had the biggest goal-hanger in the whole of Kingfield. Jamie knew he'd be in the box.

He curled in a cross and watched as his ball bent perfectly towards Alex, who was standing practically on the goal-line. He couldn't miss.

A small but purposeful jerk of Alex Marcusfield's head and the ball was in the net.

UNDER 14s B TEAM MATCH
KINGFIELD 1   ST ANTHONY'S 0
MARCUSFIELD, 7

Alex ran straight over to Jamie. He was ecstatic at having scored so early.

Jamie had his left fist clenched. What a start! He'd already done more in the first ten minutes of this game than he'd done in the whole of the last term's trial.

"What a goal!" shouted Marcusfield.

Jamie gave him a high-five. "Just get in the positions, Alex," he said. "I'll find you every time."

Jamie was sure that if he got the ball, that second goal wouldn't be far away. He already knew he could skin this Number Two.

But not everyone was as focused as Jamie. As the game went on, Kingfield's confidence started to turn into complacency.

Up front, Alex Marcusfield was being his usual greedy

self, constantly ignoring Jamie – who was in loads of space – to take on impossible shots from impossible positions. Meanwhile, at the back, the defenders were trying flamboyant flicks when they should have been keeping things nice and simple.

Kingfield paid the inevitable price when their goalkeeper and centre-half both went for the same ball and ended up bumping into each other.

The St Antony's forward couldn't believe his luck and just slotted the ball into the empty net.

UNDER 14s B TEAM MATCH
KINGFIELD 1   **ST ANTHONY'S 1**
MARCUSFIELD, 7   HUMPHRIES, 22

It was an embarrassing goal to concede. All Kingfield's – and Jamie's – good work had been undone by one stupid mistake.

Jamie could feel his cheeks burning with frustration. His teeth were beginning to grind together.

He strode over to take the centre with Alex Marcusfield. Marcusfield called Jamie closer.

"Tap it to me quickly and I'll have a shot from here," he whispered.

"No – you've had enough shots, Alex," Jamie replied.

He was ten times the player that Alex Marcusfield could ever be. "You pass it to me."

Like a dog that had been told off, Marcusfield bowed his head and obeyed his orders, touching the centre towards Jamie.

Then something very special happened.

If anyone had been watching the game at this point, they would have seen a small, pale, thin Number Eleven – with strawberry blond hair – burn a hole right through the heart of the St Antony's team. And this was straight from the kick-off!

Slaloming in and out of desperate tackles, Jamie's feet wove a spell as they sped forward.

Soon, he'd single-handedly beaten practically all the defenders St Antony's had on the pitch. Now he was through, one-on-one with the goalkeeper.

Marcusfield was desperately calling for the ball but Jamie couldn't hear him. Or at least he wasn't listening.

Jamie looked at the keeper and drew his foot back for a venomous strike. Then, at the very last minute, just as his boot was about to swipe through the ball, he checked and stopped dead.

The goalkeeper had gone for it though. He'd bought the dummy and dived.

For a second Jamie felt like the only player on the pitch. There he was, all alone, in front of an empty goal with the ball at his feet and the goalkeeper left sprawled on the ground. There was nothing left to do but pass it into the net.

UNDER 14s B TEAM MATCH
KINGFIELD 2   **ST ANTHONY'S 1**
MARCUSFIELD, 7   HUMPHRIES, 22
JOHNSON 24

It was 2 – 1 to Kingfield, thanks to the best goal Jamie had ever scored.

His teammates ran over to congratulate him, slapping his back, shaking his hand and, in Tesh's case, kissing him on the forehead! But apart from a proud smile, Jamie kept his own celebrations to a minimum. He knew it looked more classy that way.

As he jogged back to the halfway line for the restart Jamie couldn't help thinking to himself: I hope Hitchcock tells Marsden about that one!

But this game wasn't over yet.

As soon as they went back in front, Kingfield sat back trying to protect their lead. They were inviting pressure on to themselves.

It was driving Jamie mad. He hadn't scored the goal of

his life to see the rest of his team throw it away.

"Oi! Come on!" he shouted to his teammates. "We want this game! Let's keep the ball, yeah?"

Jamie could see what they were doing wrong. They were dropping too deep. Jamie knew that sometimes attack was the best form of defence. The problem was that he was the only one that knew it.

Jamie remembered what Kenny's book had said about a winger's role when his team didn't have possession. He kept working hard and tracking his man and, with twenty minutes left on the clock, he managed to tackle one of the St Antony's centre-halves deep inside their territory.

It was an opportunity for a quick break and a chance to score the decisive third goal to seal the game. Jamie passed to Alex Marcusfield and tore into the box for the return.

"YES!" he shouted as he ran.

All Marcusfield had to do was pass the ball back to him and Jamie could finish it there and then.

But the pass didn't come. Marcusfield was trying to take on the last defender. But why?

"Pass it! I'm in!" ordered Jamie but, head down, Marcusfield just kept dribbling, one way then the other, but never making any progress. In the end, the defender worked out what he was doing and got his foot in to take the ball away. To make it even worse, Marcusfield then gave away a foul by tugging the defender back.

Because of hogging the ball in front of goal, Marcusfield had managed to turn a match-winning opening into a free-kick for the opposition.

Jamie charged up to Marcusfield.

"Why can't you just pass the ball?" he roared in Marcusfield's face.

He was so angry. He kicked the ball away in disgust.

Unfortunately for Jamie, though, he belted the ball right in the direction from which Mr Hitchcock was running.

The ball flew smack bang into Mr Hitchcock's face, sending his glasses flying.

Jamie almost swallowed his tongue. He couldn't believe it!

As Mr Hitchcock scrabbled around on the ground to find his lenses and put them back in his glasses, players from both sides started to laugh. Jamie thought he'd better go and apologize.

Hitchcock was kneeling down, trying to bend his glasses back into shape. Jamie put his palm on Hitchcock's shoulder.

"Sorry, sir. That was a complete mistake."

"You're right," said Hitchcock, swatting Jamie's hand away as he stood up. "It was a very big mistake."

And with that, Hitchcock brought a red card out of his pocket and pointed very dramatically to the changing rooms.

"Ref!" appealed Jamie. "Ref, what are you doing? I didn't mean to kick it at you! I just had an argument with my teammate. You can't send me off for that."

"I just have."

UNDER 14s B TEAM MATCH
KINGFIELD 2   **ST ANTHONY'S 1**
MARCUSFIELD, 7   HUMPHRIES, 22
JOHNSON, 24
JOHNSON SENT OFF, 63

Jamie sat in the changing room by himself, trying to work out what had just happened. He could hear the shouts from the games still going on outside but he was helpless to do anything.

He knew he was the best player on that pitch by an absolute mile but he'd managed to go from hero to zero in the space of one stupid kick.

Hitchcock wouldn't tell Marsden about Jamie's brilliant goal or the fact that he'd set up the first. All he would say was that Jamie Johnson had gone psycho again and got himself sent off.

Jamie punched his fist into the wall so hard his

knuckles started to bleed.

Why did he always ruin things for himself?

22
Living for the Weekend

Friday 8 September

Jamie grabbed his bag and headed out for the weekend. It couldn't come soon enough.

The first week back at school after the holidays always seemed like it had dragged on for a year. He'd had one bit of good news when Garrick had given him a B+ for his story about Mike's injury – *Nice shades of light and dark*, he'd written at the bottom. That would keep his mum happy. But for Jamie, the week had been pretty depressing.

The fact that the B's had held on to win 2 – 1 hadn't given him much joy. He couldn't get his sending-off out of his mind. And every time he saw Alex Marcusfield, he immediately felt angry again.

If the selfish idiot had just passed the ball, Jamie would have scored his second goal and the whole year would have been talking about how good he was instead of asking why he kept going mental when he played football. He couldn't even talk to Jack about it. She was still ignoring him and spending all her time with Nicki. They'd never had a row last as long as this before.

"Hey, Jamie!" Ollie shouted to him by the lockers, "Come over here."

Ollie was standing with Jess Conners, one of fittest girls in the year. How did he always get in with the fit ones?

"Jamie, mate, I'm having a boys' night at mine tomorrow and then we're going to meet up with Jess and her lot later. You in?" he asked.

"Yeah, I should be up for that," said Jamie.

If he needed something to distract him from the sending-off, Jess Conners would do just the trick!

On Saturday afternoon Jamie texted Jack. It was time to sort this – whatever *this* was – out. He wanted to get the words right and ended up changing the message about eight times before he sent it.

He eventually settled on: Hey Jack! Remember me?! Really sorry 4 whatever I've done! U wanna hang out 2day?

Jamie had decided that even though he might get to see Jess Conners if he went to the party, what he really wanted to do was just chill with Jack – like any normal Saturday.

But Jack never responded to the text.

"All right, Jamie – come in!" said Ollie, slapping his arm around Jamie's back. He seemed even louder and happier than normal.

"We're all in the attic," he said over his shoulder as he bounded up the stairs. "It's going to be a big night."

Jamie followed. As he walked through the door into the attic, his eyes lit up. There, right before his eyes, were some of the fittest girls on TV.

OK, so they were in glossy magazines rather than there in the flesh . . . but it was a good start.

The room was pumping with hip-hop. A couple of Ollie's mates who Jamie didn't know were playing a football game against each other on the computer but most of the others were fully concentrated on the magazines on the floor.

"Don't let me interrupt you, boys!" said Jamie, kneeling to take his place in the row of admirers. They were looking at pictures of all the soap and pop stars at the latest glitzy parties.

Jamie couldn't believe girls like that actually existed. They were so fit.

He tried to imagine what would happen if he ever got

the chance to actually talk to a girl like that. He'd definitely muck it up!

"Let's have a bundle!" shouted Ollie, with a mischievous smile. He turned the music up even louder so the speakers started to vibrate and downed a can of Red Bull. "Come on, who's up for it?"

"Nah, I've got a better idea," Tesh said. "What about Truth or Dare?"

There were seven or eight of them. They all got round in a circle, including the ones Jamie didn't know. They must have been Ollie's mates from outside school.

"Right, Jamie's up first," announced Ollie.

"Ah, give me a break," said Jamie. "I've only just got here!"

"Exactly. Last in, first up. Right, the question is: you and Jack, what's the story there? Don't tell me you're just mates. Truth or Dare?"

Jamie felt his chest tighten. He should have expected that one. None of the others had a girl as a really close friend, so they were always trying to get the goss on him and Jack, find out what was "really going on".

The others were all staring expectantly at him.

"OK. . ." said Jamie, trying to buy some time. "So what's the dare?"

"Eat five slices of pizza and down two cans of Red Bull . . . in three minutes."

Ollie handed Jamie the cans and a box of pizza. Jamie opened it. It was Hawaiian – his worst type of pizza.

"I can't do that! I'll be sick – you know I will," Jamie protested.

"My bro' can do it," said Ollie proudly. "But fine, if you don't like the dare, do the truth."

"OK, fine, I'll do the dare," said Jamie. He didn't want the others to think he was a lightweight. So, without thinking any more, he started to stuff his face. He pushed two whole slices of pizza down his mouth and took a massive swig of Red Bull.

All the boys were cheering and clapping their hands as Jamie did his best to force the food down. It was disgusting though, and after about two and a half minutes, one of the bits of sweetcorn got stuck in Jamie's throat and he had to cough some of it back up.

"OK, time's up," said Tesh. "Unlucky, good effort."

"Ah, come on," Jamie appealed. "I've done four slices and both cans. That's enough, isn't it?"

"Sorry, mate," said Tesh. "The dare wasn't completed. That means it's the truth."

"Yup, the truth it is," Ollie chipped in. "Let's have it, then."

Jamie took another gulp of Red Bull. He began to see things in a different way. He may as well just tell them what they wanted to hear. They would never believe them if he told them anything else, anyway.

"OK," said Jamie. "Well, we're basically just friends these days but. . ." He paused to add suspense. "Obviously there've been a few kisses here and there. . ."

"I knew it!" said Ollie triumphantly, pointing at Jamie. "You're a dark horse, you are!"

Jamie smiled and comforted himself with the thought that, strictly speaking, it was the truth The fact that they were pretend kisses, when they were about six, was beside the point.

"I bet that's not it either, is it, Johnson?" said Ollie. "How far have you two gone, then?"

Jamie could feel his heart pumping faster and his ears starting to go red. He didn't like talking about Jack like this.

Lots more truths, dares and Red Bulls followed over the next couple of hours.

They were all pretty hyper by the time Ollie jumped to his feet and said: "Right – let's call the girls. I reckon we're ready for them now."

But Jamie wasn't ready for anything. In fact, at exactly that moment he felt a swell of sickness rush through his body like an evil tidal wave. There was no way he'd impress Jess in this state.

Even if he managed to kiss her – which was highly unlikely – he'd probably just end up being sick in her mouth.

He quickly made up some excuse about having another party to go to and left. He wanted to run home but he got really bad cramp. He could hear all the Red Bull swishing about in his stomach, all the way back.

23

The Morning After

Sunday 10 September

Jamie opened his eyes. Then he closed them. He'd hardly slept all night. He'd just lain there staring at the ceiling. Even though his body was tired, his mind had kept running around in circles while his heart had kept beating faster and faster.

He'd even started thinking about his dad, which didn't help at all.

He'd probably had about two hours of sleep all night. Now he felt horrendous. And when he tried to get up everything got worse, much worse.

He suddenly felt an unstoppable surge rise up from his stomach towards his throat. He ran to the sink and watched the sick shoot out of his mouth all in one go.

It tasted of Red Bull and looked like chewed-up pizza. Bits of pineapple and sweetcorn were getting stuck around the plughole. He had to push them down through the gaps with his finger. It was rank.

"All right, Jamie?" said Quincy Oromuyi when Jamie arrived at Sunningdale for training with the Firsts. "Was it a big one last night, by any chance? Look at the state of you!"

Jamie forced a smile but he didn't answer the question. His ears were still ringing from the sound of the music in Ollie's attic. His mouth felt dry and his stomach ached.

And this was *before* training.

It turned out to be the worst session that Jamie had played with the Firsts. When he wanted to control the ball, it bounced off him. When he wanted to pass it, he miscued it. When he wanted to take someone on for pace, his legs felt heavy. And when he wanted to track back, he couldn't keep up. He was like Superman without his powers.

Jamie knew that it was all down to the fact that he'd completely overdone it last night. He'd been trying to show off in front of the boys but he'd ended up wasting a whole training session because of it.

His body had no more energy left in it, his brain had

turned to sponge and he could still taste the sick at the back of his throat. Jamie could hardly remember what it was like to feel normal.

On his way home, Jamie got out his mobile to call Jack. He really needed a lift. Someone to talk to.

As he dialled the number, he rehearsed what he was going to say. He could be playful: "Hi, Jack, are you still mad with me?" Or maybe more apologetic: "Hi, Jack. Listen, I'm sorry. . ."

But the call just went straight to answerphone.

Jack's cheerful voice clicked into action:

"Unlucky! I'm not around. Leave a message and, if I like you, I'll call you back. See ya!"

Jamie smiled when he heard Jack's voice. But it was a sad smile.

He'd already had his dad walk out of his life without explaining. He couldn't bear the thought of losing Jack too.

(24)

Big Mouth

Monday 11 September

After assembly, Jamie caught up with Ollie and Tesh. He hadn't spoken to them since his sharp exit on Saturday night. He wanted to get the low-down on what had happened after he'd left.

"Here he is," said Ollie, with a smile. "Did you go to your *other* party?"

"Nah, I was getting a bit knackered and I had a footy game on Sunday so I called it a night," Jamie managed to pull from somewhere. He'd completely forgotten telling them that he was going to another party. "What about you? Did you meet up with the girls, by the way?"

"You left too early, man. The girls came round and Tesh got off with Steph Thompson!"

Jamie switched his eyes to a proud-looking Tesh, who nodded to confirm the deed.

"Ah, what I would give for that!" said Jamie, shaking his head. "Why do I always miss the good stuff?"

"Don't be greedy, Johnson," said Ollie, flicking his eyes in Jack's direction. She was walking across the assembly hall on her way to lessons. She gave Jamie a quick glance but her face stayed cold. Then she looked away.

She'd put some highlights in her hair. She looked nice.

At first Jamie didn't know what Ollie was going on about. Then he remembered what he'd told them about him and Jack.

"You know what?" said Ollie, looking around shiftily, trying his best to lower his booming voice. "She still fancies you. I reckon you could get quite far with her. You should go for it!"

He gave Jamie a little punch of encouragement on his shoulder.

"Get off," laughed Jamie. "And how do you know I haven't already?"

It was too late for Jamie to own up now. And anyway, Ollie seemed pretty jealous, so it was worth keeping it going just for that. They carried on laughing about it as they headed for maths.

The only problem was that someone behind Jamie, Ollie and Tesh had heard their whole conversation and didn't find it funny at all.

25
Talent, not Temper

Jamie's heart stopped. He'd checked the list for the B team twice. His name wasn't there. Hitchcock must have told Marsden that Jamie was too much of a liability to have in *any* Kingfield team. He'd been dropped.

And to make matters even worse, the games tomorrow were against The Grove, Jamie's old school. How would he be able to tell all the people he knew at The Grove that he'd gone from being practically the best player there to not even being able to get into Kingfield's B team?

At the age of thirteen, Jamie's football career was falling apart. How much worse could things get? Maybe he should just give it up. Stop playing altogether. Maybe that was the answer.

As he went to leave, his eyes quickly scanned though the A team.

And then Jamie saw something incredible.

There, at the bottom of the A team list, next to the number eleven, was his name. Jamie Johnson.

Kingfield V The Grove
Team list
1. Rob Jackson
2. Jay Rawal
3. Steve Robinson
4. Ollie Walsh
5. Dillon Simmonds (c)
6. Phil Kaye
7. Scott Newton
8. Jermaine Harley
9. Ashish Khan
10. Jason Inglethorpe
11. Jamie Johnson

Subs: Mo Hussein, Alex Marcusfield.

Team meeting in my office during break

Jamie looked around. He thought it might be a trick. He thought Dillon might come out from a doorway and start laughing, asking him how he could possibly think that he'd be in the A's. But there was no sign of him.

Jamie felt a flash of excitement sizzle through him.

Then someone tapped him on the shoulder.

"Can we have a quick chat, Jamie?"

It was Marsden. He was pointing to the staff room.

Jamie had never been into the staff room before.

The first thing that struck him was the smoke – it reeked of cigarettes.

"Take a seat, Jamie," said Mr Marsden, as he wandered towards the drinks machine. "Coffee?" he enquired.

"Oh – no thanks," said Jamie. He felt a bit nervous, as if he was somewhere he shouldn't be.

"I take it you've seen the team list for tomorrow, then?" said Marsden as he returned with a cup of coffee that was so hot you could see the steam rising from it.

"Yes. Thank you so much, sir."

"Don't thank me, Jamie. I've picked you because I think we've got a better chance of winning the game with you in the side – no other reason."

Jamie fought the smile that was making a bid to take over his face.

"But I'm taking a risk here, Jamie," said Marsden, taking a gulp of coffee. Jamie hated coffee.

"I know, sir."

"I'm not going to beat around the bush with you, Jamie. You've clearly got an issue with your anger and that's something you are going to have to address and deal with in your own time.

"I'm not saying it's a bad thing to have that fire inside you, but you've got to harness it and use it to your advantage – not let it rule you. Don't make me regret this, Jamie."

"I won't, sir. I promise I won't let you down."

"All right, then. Just make sure you show me the talent tomorrow, not the temper."

As he left the staff room, Jamie felt like he was six-feet tall. He couldn't wait to line up against his old teammates from The Grove. And he couldn't wait to see Dillon's face when he found out that Jamie was in the A's!

Meanwhile, Pete Marsden took a final sip of coffee from his mug and laid it on the table beside him. He was watching very closely as his latest recruit to the A team walked away.

There was something about Jamie Johnson's balance, something about the way he moved, even when he walked, that was different. It was natural . . . instinctive.

26

It Only Takes a Second

A strange thing happened to Jamie sometimes. When he got really good news, as well as being happy, every so often it made him feel a bit sad at the same time.

He could remember that when he lived in Grove Avenue with his mum and his dad he was happy the whole time. He could remember when his dad used to take him for walks in Sunningdale when he was really young. That was when he first learned to kick a football. In those days, he only ever smiled.

But recently he'd found that for no particular reason, and often without warning, he might lose his temper really badly or else suddenly start to feel down.

He knew it was weird and he didn't know why it happened. But it was happening again today.

He'd just been named in the A team. The A team! It was what he'd been working towards every day for the last two months. And yet, just now, right at the moment he'd actually achieved it, somewhere inside him he felt an emptiness. And he didn't know how to fill it.

Maybe if he told Mike the news he'd snap out of it. He knew if Mike was happy, he'd feel it too. He headed straight over to see him after school.

"Guess what?" said Jamie, standing behind Mike, who was watching football on TV.

"What's up, JJ?"

"Mike, you are looking at the new Kingfield A team left-winger," said Jamie proudly.

"Oh, fantastic, mate! Well done!" Mike stood up to firmly shake Jamie's hand. He had such a big smile. He looked even more proud than Jamie.

"Yup," said Jamie. "I'll be wearing the Number Eleven shirt tomorrow for my debut. And guess who we're playing? The Grove!"

"What a game to get you started, JJ! Just give it

everything you've got – for the whole ninety minutes. Don't forget, one kick of the ball can change a game, like that," he said, clicking his fingers. "It only takes a second to score a goal.

"And don't over-analyse things either. You know you've got the talent – you've always had the talent – just go where it leads you."

"Good shout, Mike," said Jamie, dropping to the floor for an impromptu set of press-ups. He had to get rid of some of his nervous energy.

"What does Jack reckon then, JJ? She's your biggest fan, isn't she?"

Jamie stopped doing his press-ups. When he heard Jack's name, that empty feeling from earlier came back. Except this time Jamie knew why he was feeling it: he wanted to share this with her.

And he couldn't.

27
Sorry

There, standing in the doorway with her hands on hips, was Jack.

Instead of training with the Firsts tonight Jamie had gone round to hers. He had to have it out with her sooner or later. It was the only way they might get back to normal.

"What do you want, Johnson?" she shouted.

"I want to be your mate again," said Jamie, breaking into a nervous grin. "I'm sorry I didn't call you when you got back from holiday but it's not the end of the world, is it? Can't we just forget it and go and grab a milkshake?"

"More like so you can grab a feel. Isn't that what you want to do?"

Jamie felt his stomach drop right through his body.

"What are you talking about, Jack?"

"I know what you and Ollie said about me," Jack shot back. "I'm not an idiot, Jamie. Nicki heard the whole thing. It's disgusting. And I thought you were different!"

Her! Of course it was her. Jamie could imagine how Nicki had made it sound to Jack. Like he'd just been playing her the whole time.

He had to think quickly. He had to turn this around.

"Oh, that," he said, trying to sound calm. "Listen, Jack, I may as well come clean. . . The thing is, Ollie really fancies you so he's jealous of me 'cos we are – or were – so . . . you know . . . close. I just wanted to wind him up a bit to make him jealous. That's all it was. Honest. I didn't know you'd find out. I'm sorry."

"And what if I hadn't found out? That would have been OK then, would it?"

"No, that's not what I'm saying—"

"What's happened to you, Jamie? I go away for a few weeks and when I come back it's like I don't exist any more. Like you couldn't . . . care less about me. How do you think that makes me feel? Like there's no point in us being friends any more. *That's* how it makes me feel."

Jamie was getting so frustrated. There were so many things he wanted to say to Jack. He wanted to tell her to stop. That she was his best friend. That she'd always be his best friend. That he needed her.

But Jack was angry too. Jamie knew that when she was like this there was no way of talking her round. He had to leave. Otherwise he'd lose his temper and it would get even worse. He could feel it.

"Fair enough," said Jamie. "Your choice."

He was trying to keep himself calm but he felt like kicking the gate to her house right off its hinges.

As he started to walk away, Jamie expected to hear the door slam shut behind him. But he didn't. Instead, he heard a sound he'd never heard before: Jack crying.

Her loud, angry shouts had been replaced by soft, sad tears.

Jamie turned and looked at his best friend. He couldn't believe he'd caused her to be in this state.

Were football and his other mates more important than Jack? Maybe that was how he'd been acting.

"Get lost, Jamie, go away!" she screamed, as he walked towards her.

But he kept on walking and put his arm around her.

"Get lost, I said," she roared, hitting him hard in the chest, trying desperately to quell her tears. "Don't touch me."

"I'm so sorry, Jack," said Jamie. "Please don't cry."

"I hate you, Jamie Johnson."

"I know . . . and I'm sorry," he said softly. "I'm an

idiot. But you can't stay mad at me for ever."

"Yes, I can!" said Jack, hitting him hard in the chest again. For a second Jamie thought he saw the beginnings of a smile start to replace the frown on her face.

"That's it," he said. "Hit me. I deserve it. Not *too* hard, though!"

Now Jack was laughing as well as crying. He'd missed her laugh.

"I'll hit you as hard as I want, GINGE!" she shouted, snivelling back her tears, while her burst of punches came to an end.

As she lifted her head up from his chest and started to mess up his hair, their noses brushed together for a second.

"Never let me down again," Jack said.

"I won't," he whispered and they gave each other a big bear hug.

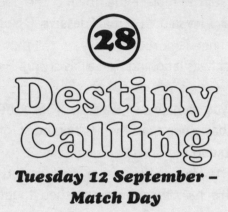

28

Destiny Calling

Tuesday 12 September – Match Day

"Jamie, get up! It's gone 8.15. We're late!"

"What?" said Jamie vacantly. For a second he wasn't sure where he was. He'd been in a really deep sleep.

"I overslept," shouted Jamie's mum, scampering around in the hallway. "We're really late."

Jamie could hear his mum giggling. She hadn't giggled in years. But what was she doing giggling when he was late for school on the day he was going to play the biggest match of his life?

"MUM!! I can't be late today!" he bellowed as he

scrambled out of bed and started to get dressed. His fingers were shaking as he tried to do up the buttons on his shirt. He'd only just got up and he was already nervous.

"I haven't even got time for breakfast now!" he shouted. "I need energy today. I was going to have eggs on toast!"

Jamie's mum didn't reply. He was sure he could hear her talking to someone. He charged down the stairs to see what was going on.

His mum was in the hall getting ready for work. There was a man there with her, helping her keep her balance as she put on her shoes.

She looked up and saw Jamie, who'd stopped halfway down the stairs.

"Morning, love," she said with an unusually broad smile. "Oh, this is Jeremy, by the way."

"Hello, Jamie," said the man. He sounded very polite. "I've heard a lot about you from your mum. I hear there's a big soccer game on this afternoon."

"All right," said Jamie. He knew that this must be the guy who picked his mum up for work everyday. He didn't normally come in the house, though.

Still, Jamie had more important things on his mind than small-talk with strangers. "Mum, where's my kit?" he asked.

"It's by the door, Jamie. I ironed it for you last night. Now good luck!" she said, squashing his cheeks together and kissing him on the forehead.

"Goodbye, Jamie. Very nice to meet you," said Jeremy as they left for work.

"Whatever," Jamie mumbled under his breath as he poured himself a bowl of cereal. He had to get it down his throat quickly. It wasn't good for his digestion but he needed to start loading his body with carbs.

At the end of assembly, Mr Patten, Kingfield's head teacher, turned his attention to the fixtures with The Grove.

"And finally," he said, glancing down at a piece of paper in front of him, "our Under Twelves, Thirteens, Fourteens and the First Eleven have games against The Grove School this afternoon. Traditionally, our matches against The Grove are amongst the most . . . closely contested of the football calendar."

A murmur went around the assembly hall. Everyone knew what Mr Patten was talking about. The two schools were big rivals. They pretty much hated each other. After their game last year, Jamie had had a bruise on his shin for about two weeks where Dillon had kicked him. He wasn't sure how he felt about playing on the same side as Dillon today. Still, Ollie was in the team too, and he was a brilliant midfielder to play with.

"Remember our school motto," continued Mr Patten, a steeliness in his voice now. "'*Rise to the Challenge*'.

"To everyone representing Kingfield today, I say this." He lowered his glasses to make direct eye contact with his students. "Rise to *this* challenge. Good luck to you all."

Jack jabbed her elbow into Jamie's ribs and smiled. Jamie grinned. He glanced across to look at Nicki who was sitting where she used sit in the next row. Jamie was so happy to have his best mate back.

Pride, nerves and excitement were all washing over him at the same time. He felt as though Mr Patten had been talking just to him. He couldn't believe that his first game for the A's was going to be against his old team!

During history, Jamie found it really difficult to focus on the lesson. Just keeping still was taking up most of his concentration. His legs seemed to have a mind of their own and his feet were bouncing up and down under the desk as if they were connected to an electric current. He had to try and keep some of this energy for the match!

Just before the end of the lesson, Mr Marsden popped his head around the door. After asking permission from Miss Claunt, he made a quick announcement to the class.

"Could my A team boys – that's Ollie, Jamie and Ashish – meet me in my office at break, please," he said. "Thanks and sorry to interrupt, Miss Claunt."

Ollie and Jamie exchanged smiles. They were classmates now but in a couple of hours they would be teammates.

㉙
Team-talk

Mr Marsden greeted each of his players with a nod as they filed in and leaned against the walls of his small, rectangular office.

He'd already set up the whiteboard to show the boys the formation he wanted to use that afternoon. He had eleven magnetic counters to represent each one of his players.

Jamie looked around the room and studied all the posters of different sports on the walls. He was taking everything in. His eyes were wide and his ears were sharp.

"Morning, lads, hope everyone's feeling good," Marsden said. "There's a lot of ability in this room and I'm very confident that we'll demonstrate that later on today.

"I've laid out the formation on the whiteboard. You'll see it's a 4 – 4 – 2 but I want it to be a 4 – 4 – 2 that plays to our strengths."

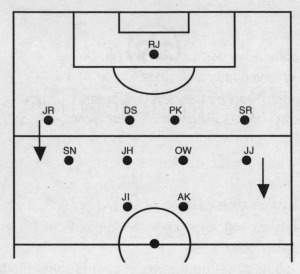

Marsden went through his plans for the defence and the midfield, giving each player their own set of individual instructions. Then he placed his finger on the fourth midfield counter, the one on the left-hand side.

"As you all know, I've called up Jamie Johnson," he said. "Jamie's going to play on the left wing for us."

Jamie could feel his cheeks burning as Mr Marsden mentioned his name. He really liked the way that Mr Marsden was talking about him as if he were a new signing.

"Jamie should give us a bit more pace and invention going forward," he continued. "His job is to provide the ammunition for Ashish and Jason up front.

"Ashish and Jason, make sure you stay close, play as a partnership and don't be afraid to shoot. That goes for everybody. If we don't shoot, we can't score.

"Everyone happy with that?"

"Yes, sir," replied the boys collectively.

"Right – any questions?"

"Sir – what are we going to do about Shaun McGiven?" asked Steve Robinson, the left full-back.

Jamie had wondered how long it would be before McGiven's name was mentioned.

Everyone in the area knew about McGiven – but no one better than Jamie. He'd played alongside him for The Grove for the last five years. He was easily the best striker Jamie had ever played with. He was a natural predator, born to score goals. He seemed to have a map of the pitch programmed into his head. He always knew where the goal was, without having to look.

He was, without doubt, The Grove's most powerful weapon. Most teams generally felt they had done a good job on him if he only scored two goals in a match. That's how good he was.

"Good question, Steve – I'm glad you asked that," said Marsden, before taking a gulp of coffee from his mug.

"Let me turn the question around though: how are they going to deal with us?"

Mr Marsden's fist was clenched and his knuckles had gone white.

"McGiven's a good player. We need to deal with him, of course we do. So talk to each other and make sure he's always picked up.

"But we are *not* going to play this game trying to stop The Grove. They are going to have to stop us. Agreed?"

"Agreed!"

㉚ Pre-match

For once, the dinner ladies had got it right. Pasta was a good pre-match meal.

The only problem was that Jamie wasn't hungry. And Jack wasn't helping much either.

"You'll have to score today," she said, giving Jamie a shoulder-barge to make the spaghetti slip off his fork again. "You know all the best players score on their debuts! And they always score against their old teams. So actually you've got to score two! And I'll be there to see it."

Jamie put down his fork. He appreciated the fact that people were expecting him to make a big impression but, at the same time, it piled on the pressure. He just hoped he could deliver.

Jamie grabbed a banana and made his way down to the changing rooms, picking up his sports bag along the way. "Come on!" he ordered himself through clenched teeth.

He did some bicep crunches with his sports bag as he walked. He could feel the blood surging through his veins. The bag was light as he lifted it to his chest. He felt stronger than he ever had before.

The changing room was buzzing with excitement. Most of the boys had already started to get changed.

It was strange, because although Jamie knew everyone in the team, he really felt like a new boy again.

"All right, Jamie," said Jason Inglethorpe, shaking his hand. "You whip in the crosses to me and Ash; we'll do the rest."

"Cool. That's what I'm here for," replied Jamie, shaking his hand firmly. "If you get some space, I'll find you."

Jamie went and sat down next to Ollie. He opened his bag and pulled out his kit. Blue shirt, white shorts and blue socks. He'd waited long enough to get his hands on this kit. He brought the shirt close to his nose. It smelled fresh and clean. He turned it around and traced his fingers over the number eleven on the back. Eleven. Jamie Johnson's number.

He got changed and did some quick hamstring

stretches before going to put his boots on. He couldn't see them in his bag but he knew they would be in there somewhere.

He did the same thing with his keys the whole time. They were always at the bottom.

Jamie told himself to stay calm but he could feel his forehead starting to burn. The more he searched for his boots, the less sure he was that they were actually there. But they had to be. Where else could they be?

Now his hands were scraping around the corner of the bag, right to the plastic lining. Still they found nothing.

"Where the hell are they?" Jamie shouted to himself above the rest of the noise in the dressing room. He tipped the whole bag upside down. His hands were trembling.

Some old socks and a T-shirt fell out. But no boots.

Jamie could feel freezing little pockets of sweat start to form down his spine.

He kicked his bag as hard as he could across the room.

"Why?" he shouted.

The rest of the boys stopped talking. They looked at Jamie. He was completely red in the face.

"You all right, mate?" asked Ollie.

Jamie didn't answer. He could feel his anger starting to burn up inside him.

"Whassup, Ginge?" said Dillon, kicking the bag back

at Jamie. "Don't be a cry baby. You're with the big boys now."

Seeing the evil in Dillon's eyes told Jamie everything he needed to know. Suddenly it all made sense.

Jamie had left his sports bag in the assembly hall while he was having lunch. Dillon must have nicked his boots then. He would do anything just to stop Jamie playing in the A's.

"Give me my boots!" demanded Jamie, squaring up to Dillon. "I want them now."

His voice was starting to sound wild. He had too much anger and worry to hold it all in.

"Oh, it's my fault, now?" Dillon laughed. "Grow up, Cry-Baby. Don't blame me for everything that goes wrong in your whole life – like the fact that you haven't got a dad."

That was it. Jamie had had enough. He didn't care how big a game it was or how much work he'd put into getting here. He didn't have to take this from anyone. Least of all from that idiot.

If Dillon hated him so much that he would steal boots from his own teammate, then he could have his stupid way.

Jamie was off.

㉛
Big Boots
to Fill

"Where are you off to in such a hurry, Jamie? We're kicking off in fifteen minutes," said Marsden, blocking Jamie's path in the corridor.

"I'm not playing, sir," said Jamie stubbornly.

"What are you talking about? Of course you're playing, Jamie!"

"Simmonds has stolen my boots. I'm not playing in any team he's in."

"I see," said Mr Marsden, tilting his head slightly. "I take it you're quite sure about that?"

Jamie nodded.

Mr Marsden went quiet for a second. Then he said:

"OK, well, clearly we'll have to sort this out later; it's too close to kick-off now. What we've got to do now is find you a new pair of boots – quickly."

He pointed to his office.

"No, sir. I'm not. . ."

"Jamie, we haven't got time for this. Get in here now."

By the time Jamie got back to the changing room, the noisy anticipation that had filled it earlier had gone. Everyone was already outside warming up.

Jamie bent down to put on the boots that Marsden had found in the lost property bin. They were way too big, and they looked about fifty years old.

There was no way he'd be able to play well in them. He wouldn't even be able to feel the ball.

Jamie hated Dillon more than anyone in the world. Some of the teachers went easy on him because he had issues at home. But that didn't give him the right to go around stealing other people's things.

Jamie would never forgive him for this. Ever.

32
Kick-off

By the time Jamie hesitantly walked out on to the pitch, there were only a couple of minutes left before kick-off.

Dillon was giving his own brand of pre-match team-talk.

"This is it, lads," he said aggressively. "We can't let this bunch of muppets come here and beat us on our own turf. Let's go in hard and show 'em what we're made of."

Jamie wasn't listening. He couldn't care less what that thick bully had to say. Instead, he let his eyes wander towards the Grove team, who were all in a huddle on the centre circle. He recognized all the faces and noticed how much they had all grown since last year. He would've shaken hands with a few of them but none of them acknowledged him.

Beyond them and along the line of people that had

gathered to watch the game, Jamie saw Mike at the far end of the pitch.

Mike gave him the thumbs up and Jamie raised a wave and a faint smile but, inside, his heart was sinking.

He couldn't believe that his own captain would steal his boots on the day of the biggest game of his life.

For the first time he could ever remember, Jamie felt he didn't belong on a football pitch. He felt like a dolphin in the desert.

Just before the kick-off, Bryn Staunton, the Grove captain and their hardest player, came up to Jamie. When they had been on the same side, Bryn used to protect Jamie if he was coming in for any rough treatment.

"All right, mate," said Jamie, offering his hand.

"You know we're not mates today, don't you, Jamie?" said Bryn, squeezing Jamie's hand really hard. "And I wouldn't bother trying any of your skills on me either. I know them all, remember?"

Then the match kicked off.

UNDER 14s A TEAM MATCH
KINGFIELD V THE GROVE

For the first few minutes, there was hardly any passing at all. It was all tackles and fouls, throw-ins and free-kicks.

The two teams were battling each other, not playing football.

Out on the wing, Jamie hardly got a touch of the ball. He felt so uncomfortable in these rubbish old boots. It was like he was back in the trials. He could feel that everyone was against him, willing him to fail.

The opposition hated him because he used to play for them and even his own teammates were stealing his boots. Jamie just couldn't get into the game.

The one bright spot for Kingfield was Ashish Khan. He was looking sharp, lively and quick. Whenever they got the ball to Ash's feet, he always threatened to make something happen.

Unfortunately, The Grove had noticed this too. And after ten minutes, with Ashish running full pelt at their defence, Bryn Staunton thundered into him with a horrendous challenge.

Jamie knew that in every game Bryn's plan was to clatter into the opposition's best player in the first quarter of an hour. To let him know "he was around". Bryn had obviously decided that today Ashish was his target. Not only had he charged into him, he'd then fallen with all his weight on Ash's ankle.

Even the people watching the game on the sideline cringed when it happened. It was ugly, dangerous and clearly intentional.

As Mr Marsden dashed on to the pitch to help Ashish hobble off, Bryn held his hands up in the air to acknowledge his foul. He could hardly have denied it.

The referee pulled him to one side and showed him a yellow card immediately.

But Bryn wasn't bothered. In fact, he was smiling. He'd got rid of Kingfield's most dangerous player at the cost of a booking. From his point of view, it was a good deal.

With Ash off, Kingfield lost their cutting edge and The Grove took a grip on the game. Strong and organized, they were grinding forward like an army on the attack.

Jamie was on the outside of the game, looking in.

He started to drift away from the wing, coming further infield in search of the ball.

But with Jamie more central, The Grove's right-back had a free reign down the right flank. And, in the twenty-fifth minute, he made that space count, with a strong run all the way down the line.

Jamie tried to get back at him but the right-back had had too much of a headstart.

In the end, Dillon came across from his centre-half position and slid in with a tackle. He was late though, and gave away a free-kick right on the edge of the area.

"Johnson!" Dillon shouted angrily as he got up. "Wake up, you idiot. You're playing for us, not them."

"Shut up, you thief," Jamie shouted back.

But while Dillon and Jamie were busy shouting at each other, The Grove had already taken a quick free-kick to find McGiven. With Dillon still out of position, McGiven was unmarked.

Before any of the Kingfield players had a chance to react, he'd controlled the ball with a sweet first touch and driven it along the ground into the far corner of the net.

It was in as soon as he'd struck it. They had left McGiven alone for one second and had paid the price.

UNDER 14s A TEAM MATCH
KINGFIELD   0   THE GROVE   1
KHAN OFF INJURED. 13   MCGIVEN. 27
SUB: HUSSEIN ON

Jamie hung his head. He knew everyone would blame him for letting the full-back go in the first place.

As they prepared to take the re-start, Jamie looked at the people watching the game. He wondered what they all thought of him. "Loser", probably.

Maybe he'd been fooling himself all these years. Maybe he was never as good as he thought he was. But if that was the case, had his whole life been one big lie?

Then Jamie stopped dead. He thought he'd seen a ghost.

At the end of the line of spectators, sitting patiently by itself, was the dog with the scary eyes that he'd seen in the park during the holidays. Was it on its own or was the tramp there too?

Jamie scanned the crowd and then he saw him. And he couldn't believe what he was doing.

The tramp was talking to Jamie's granddad. And Mike actually seemed relaxed about it. He didn't look scared at all. In fact, he seemed to be making notes on a pad while the tramp was talking.

But what was he writing? And why was he talking to the tramp in the first place?

Half-time Truths

UNDER 14s A TEAM MATCH
HALF-TIME
KINGFIELD 0   THE GROVE 1
MCGIVEN. 27

When the half-time whistle went, Marsden urgently called his team over to the touchline. He couldn't get them there quick enough.

Normally he was so calm and positive. But now he was angry and agitated.

"Come in, lads, come in," he shouted, gathering his players around him.

"Well, I hope you've got that out of your system," he said, looking each of his players directly in the eye as they sheepishly bit into their oranges. Jamie could see a vein throbbing in the side of Marsden's forehead.

"I'll tell you something – we're damn lucky," he carried on.

"We should be dead and buried the way we're giving away possession. We are lucky it's only 1 – 0 and we're still in it.

"If we're going to shout at each other instead of marking up when we're defending set-pieces, we've got no hope," he said, eyeing Dillon and Jamie.

"I'll tell you what. A few of you are lucky I've only got one sub left to make. If we can't turn things around, then I'll be making a change," he said, pointing to Alex Marcusfield, who was the other substitute.

As he peeled away to retake his position, Jamie wondered whether him being substituted might be the best thing for everyone. Even if it meant Marcusfield taking his place.

He just didn't feel right today. It wasn't just the boots. He was a stranger in his own body and he couldn't see what was going to change it.

As Jamie got back to his position on the wing, he saw his granddad standing on the touchline, gesturing him to come over.

There was just enough time to grab a word before kick-off.

"Mike! What are you talking to that man for?" said Jamie, staring at the tramp. "He could be dangerous."

Mike laughed. "He's not dangerous, Jamie. Well, not since I've known him!"

"You *know* him? Who is he?"

"Like I told you, Jamie. He's the best coach I ever met."

Jamie felt goose-pimples rise up all over his body. Suddenly he knew who the tramp was.

"What? *That's* Kenny Wilcox? But he's. . ."

"I know. He's gone off the rails a bit," said Mike shaking his head. "It's a tragedy really – such a loss to the game. He always did have a bit of a drink problem . . . anyway we haven't got time for this. Kenny told me to write this down and to give it to you. It's about today's game."

Mike handed Jamie a scrap of paper. It was in Mike's handwriting but to Jamie it read just like all the drills in the book that he'd spent the whole summer practising. This is what it said:

You are a winger, so stay on the wing. Coming inside only narrows the pitch and your options. There's no need to make it complicated; stay out wide and attack your man.

Use your change of pace to unsettle him. And when you attack, do it with conviction.

"He's right, Jamie."

It was a lot for Jamie to take in: he was getting advice from a tramp who also happened to be a legendary coach.

But, in some strange way, it all seemed to make sense.

34

Chasing McGiven

Jamie did what Kenny had suggested and stayed out wide. But for the first ten minutes of the second half, the ball hardly got out of the centre circle. The midfield was so congested. Neither team were getting the ball out to the wings and without the ball, how could Jamie make a difference?

Jamie looked across to the touchline. Alex Marcusfield

was taking off his tracksuit top and Marsden was giving him instructions.

Jamie knew that Marsden had to do something to get his team back in the game, and swapping a striker for a winger might help them to nick a goal. Although it hurt more than anything to admit it, deep down, Jamie knew he would be the one to make way.

At that moment, a Kingfield attack broke down and The Grove's keeper had the ball in his hands. He assessed his options quickly and instantly punted a firm, flat kick forward.

McGiven was alert to the situation and immediately latched on to the long ball.

He'd completely broken the offside trap and was now running free towards the Kingfield goal. He could make the game safe for The Grove.

The Kingfield players gave up on chasing him; they'd never be able to stop McGiven. They all just stood and watched.

All except one.

Seeing McGiven break free had triggered Jamie to start running. It was as if a gun had gone off inside his head. He hurtled off in pursuit.

Jamie was sprinting back towards his own goal at lightning pace. He knew exactly what McGiven was going to do. He'd seen it so many times when they had played together. He could see by the shape of McGiven's body that he was going to open himself up and curl one into the far corner.

But it was too late to try and tackle him. He was already preparing to strike the ball.

McGiven hit his shot with effortless accuracy. It bent past the keeper and sailed towards the net . . . until, arriving from nowhere, Jamie flung himself at the ball, stretching his leg to its full limit, to somehow get a touch to it and flick it over the bar.

He'd anticipated where the ball was going to go and got there just in time. He'd cleared it off the line and saved a definite goal.

Jamie lay flat on the goal-line. His lungs were demanding his mouth pull in huge gulps of air. He'd sprinted nearly the entire length of the pitch to stop McGiven.

Above the sound of his own panting, Jamie was also aware of a pattering noise in the background. It was people clapping. People clapping Jamie. He felt a flutter of pride as his teammates helped him to his feet.

And on the touchline, Marsden was telling Alex Marcusfield to put his tracksuit back on.

㉟
High Hopes

Now the game started to change. Suddenly, it was Kingfield who were first to every loose ball.

Soon they won a corner and, as he sprinted over to take it, their left-winger felt that old power in his legs again.

Jamie Johnson was back. He just knew it.

Jamie placed the ball on the corner spot and took two steps back. He looked up and saw the penalty area alive with a sea of jostling bodies.

For a second Jamie imagined he was back in Sunningdale with Danny Miller and the other boys playing the Crossbar Challenge.

Stepping towards the ball, he swept his foot delicately underneath it with a smooth rhythm to produce a beautiful floating cross into the centre. It seemed to just hang in the air.

Dillon made a run from the penalty spot and leapt high to meet it. As he made contact with the ball in the air, he was about a foot above everyone else. His neck was straight and powerful and he directed a bullet of a header into the roof of the net.

GOAL!!!

UNDER 14s A TEAM MATCH
KINGFIELD 1   THE GROVE 1
SIMMONDS, 58   MCGIVEN, 27

Dillon, roaring in delight, was being mobbed in The Grove's goalmouth.

"That's what *I'm* talking about!" he was shouting.

Meanwhile, Jamie enjoyed his own private celebration by the corner flag.

"Nice one, mate!" said Ollie, hitting Jamie on the back. "Perfect corner."

"Cheers," said Jamie as the pair jogged back to their positions for the restart. "Now let's get another one."

"Come on, Kingfield!"

"Come on, The Grove!"

Both sets of supporters urged their teams on as Shaun McGiven took the centre for The Grove.

It was now a match within a match. Ten minutes remaining. 1 – 1. The next goal would win it.

Kingfield sensed the momentum was with them and pressed forward, searching for that glorious winner. But they were so keen to get the ball forward quickly, that instead of looking to pick the right passes at the right time, they started to just hump the ball upfield every time they got it.

The high, aimless balls were meat and drink for the tall boys in the Grove's back four.

"Calm down! Keep the ball!" shouted Marsden as attack after attack came to nothing.

The minutes trickled away.

Soon there were only three minutes left and Kingfield's keeper was preparing to launch one final big kick up the field.

"Give it to Jamie!" Ollie suddenly ordered the keeper. He'd seen that Jamie had found some space.

Instead of kicking it, the keeper pulled his arm back and bowled the ball out to Jamie, who had dropped short and wide to receive it.

Jamie collected the ball on the halfway line. He had it at his feet. It was now or never. He knew what he had to do.

Jamie concentrated all the power of his mind and body into one place. Then he just ran.

He instantly clicked through the gears to hit top speed. Two, three, four of the Grove players tried to stop him, but they couldn't keep up. Jamie's pace was frightening. The boots weren't holding him back any more. Nothing could hold him back now. He seemed to be going faster and faster the longer he kept the ball.

Soon he was at the edge of the area with just one man left to beat: Bryn Staunton. Jamie had seen what he'd done to Ash in the first half. But he had no fear.

Bryn thought he knew all of Jamie's skills, did he? Well, now he'd have to prove it.

Jamie ran straight towards Bryn, shaping to go on the inside. Bryn could see what Jamie was doing and moved across to cover that route to goal. But, just as Bryn committed himself, Jamie took another touch and nudged the ball down the outside instead.

Jamie's swift change of direction had destroyed Bryn. He was past him and into the area. He was through on goal!

But Bryn had no intention of allowing Jamie to get away that easily.

He turned around as quickly as he could and pulled hard at Jamie's shirt, dragging him back. They both fell to the ground at the same time.

And as they hit the deck, Bryn did something even sneakier. He made sure that he landed with his elbow in Jamie's face. He crashed his forearm across Jamie's nose. It was no mistake. He knew what he was doing.

Jamie was seething. He was furious. Not only had Bryn stopped him from scoring, he'd also tried to take him out. And to make it even worse, Bryn was just pretending nothing had happened.

Seeing Bryn get up and walk away like he hadn't done anything made something snap in Jamie.

All the anger Jamie had ever felt in his life had rolled up into one ball and turned his blood into venom.

He chased after Bryn. He was going to kick him as hard as he could.

But just as he was about to rake his studs right down the back of Bryn's ankles, Jamie's mind flashed back to the conversation he'd had with Marsden the day before.

Jamie had promised him he wouldn't let him down.

"Oi, mate," said Jamie in Bryn's ear.

"You didn't remember that trick, did you?"

Bryn turned around.

"You little. . ." he snarled, pulling back his fist to smack Jamie, but the referee quickly put his body between the two players.

He marched Bryn away to the touchline.

"That's it, Number Five, I've lost my patience with you,"

he said. "Firstly, that was a goal-scoring opportunity for Kingfield and you made no attempt to play the ball, and secondly, I have no doubt you were just about to use violent conduct.

"You're off," he said, first showing Bryn a second yellow card, and then a red.

Bryn Staunton spat on the ground. With a glare of contempt, he pointed his finger at Jamie and mouthed the word "LATER". Then he left the field.

Jamie wasn't bothered. Kingfield had a pen' and The Grove were down to ten.

36
Penalty Chance

Finally, Jamie had done his bit. He had won Kingfield a penalty single-handedly. Now he just hoped they could convert it. He was so full of anticipation. He looked around to see who was going to take it.

"Johnson!" shouted Dillon. He walked up to Jamie and shoved the ball into his stomach.

They stood looking at each other and, for a second, neither knew what to do. Jamie had his hands on the ball but was unable to accept it. Dillon was offering Jamie the ball, yet unwilling to let go.

He wanted Jamie to take the penalty? After what had happened in the trials?

Did Dillon really think Jamie was the best man to take it? Or did he just want him to make a fool of himself again?

Then again, who else was there? Jamie was the one who'd won the penalty with a run all the way from the halfway line. He was the man in form.

Jamie looked at Mr Marsden who was standing behind the goal. Marsden nodded back at him and clenched his fist.

Dillon released his grip on the ball and walked away. It was Jamie's penalty.

The referee took the ball from Jamie and planted it on the spot.

A million pictures and memories were sweeping around Jamie's mind: the trials, Kenny Wilcox, Danny Miller, Jack, Mike. He didn't want to let anyone down.

He looked around and saw the big crowd on the touchline. They were all looking at him, waiting. Everyone knew that this penalty was going to decide the match.

He saw that Kenny Wilcox was still there, standing next to Mike. Jack had arrived too and, next to them, was his mum. What was his mum doing there? Why wasn't she at work?

Jamie's heart seemed to be beating all through his body. He could feel it in his chest, in his throat and in his head.

Everything depended on him.

He had to score.

The keeper was waving his arms around above his head to put Jamie off.

The whistle went. Then silence. Everything stopped.

Jamie fixed his eye on the ball.

"Be my friend now," he whispered.

Then he stepped forward, knowing that Kingfield were just one kick – his kick – from victory.

Wallop. Jamie punched his foot firmly through the ball, sweeping it with his instep towards the top right-hand corner of the goal. He followed right through to get extra power. It whistled in search of its target.

He was sure it was in.

And it was a fine strike. But unfortunately for Jamie, the Grove keeper had guessed right.

Jamie could only watch as the keeper sprang himself high into the air. It all seemed to be happening in slow-motion.

Jamie saw the keeper extend himself to his very full length . . . the keeper shot his left arm up above his head . . . he clasped for the ball with his fingertips . . . and managed to poke it wide of the goal. It was a brilliant save.

"Yes!" bellowed Bryn Staunton from the touchline, punching the air.

"No!" fumed Mr Marsden, punching the palm of his hand.

Jamie's mum covered her face. She knew how much this meant to Jamie. Would he be able to cope with the disappointment? And would he blame her?

But if everyone thought it was over, they hadn't seen what Jamie had seen. The ball wasn't out of play; it hadn't gone much wide of the post.

Jamie set off with a huge burst of speed. He instantly found his turbo gear.

He left the defenders in his wake. It was a straight race between him and the keeper, who was scrambling towards the ball on his hands and knees.

But nothing was going to stop Jamie. He slid along the ground and got to the ball just before the keeper's desperate claw.

From an angle, he scooped the ball towards the goal with his right foot.

It bounced once.

Then it kissed the back of the net.

UNDER 14s A TEAM MATCH

KINGFIELD 2	THE GROVE 1
SIMMONDS, 58	MCGIVEN, 27
JOHNSON, 70 [+1]	

37
Walking Tall

From beneath the pile of Kingfield players who were celebrating uncontrollably on top of him, Jamie could just about make out the muffled sound of the full-time whistle.

He pulled himself away from the scrum of delight and ran over to his mum, Mike and Jack.

Jamie burst between them, roaring: "Have that!"

He'd never been this happy in his life.

Jack jumped on his back.

"I spotted you first – remember that!" she shouted, giving him a massive kiss on the cheek.

Karen Johnson was next in line to hug her son, the goal-scorer.

"You were brilliant, Jamie," she said proudly. "And

you would never have forgiven me if you'd lost, would you?"

Jamie looked up.

"Forgiven you? For what?"

"Your boots," said Karen. "I took them out of your bag to clean them last night and in all the rush this morning –"

Then it all clicked in Jamie's mind.

He looked at his boots, dangling by their laces from his mum's hand. Then he looked down at the crusty old pair that Marsden had found in lost property.

He couldn't help but laugh. Maybe he had some apologizing to do too.

"Forget it, Mum. It's fine," he said. "It didn't exactly work out too badly in the end!"

Then, from nowhere, Ollie and Jason Inglethorpe came rampaging towards Jamie.

They clasped their arms around Jamie's legs and lifted him on to their shoulders. They were singing his name.

From his lofty perch, Jamie could just make out the figure of a man and his dog walking away into the woods behind the fields. Jamie nodded towards them.

Although he couldn't see Kenny Wilcox's face, he could have sworn there was a smile etched all the way across it.

That day Kingfield School found a new hero.

But what no one knew – least of all the young footballer himself – was that this was just the start of Jamie Johnson's story.

Only the kick-off.

Interview with Dan Freedman

You've been to the World Cup twice, what was it like?

Before becoming an author, I worked as a journalist with the England Football Team. That meant living in the team hotel, having breakfast with players like Wayne Rooney and Steven Gerrard and then going to watch them train and play in the World Cup Finals. They were some of the greatest experiences of my life. I realize how lucky I was and I thought about those times a lot when I was writing this book.

Can you do all of Jamie's best moves?

Of course I can – I'm a phenomenal footballer, one of the best in the world. See, that's the good thing about being an author: you can just make stuff up.

Who are your favourite footballers at the moment?

You can't ignore Messi's majestic talent and I absolutely love the way that Xavi never ever loses the ball. Gerrard for his passion and loyalty to his club and, for the future, Jack Wilshere. So young but soooo good!

You visit lots of schools – what's the funniest question you've been asked?

Lots of kids seem fascinated to know what car I drive (a Golf, if you must know). Some ask me if I ever get bored of football (no). And one boy asked me which footballer had the biggest appetite when it came to meal times! The school visits are great fun because they are a chance for me to meet the people that I write the books for.

Who is the most famous person you've interviewed?

Take your pick: David Beckham, Cristiano Ronaldo, Sir Alex Ferguson. At the time, I had pretend that it was no big deal and that I was all cool about it but inside I was thinking: "Oh my God! I can't believe I'm interviewing him!"

So have you ever had a kick around with Wayne Rooney?

No – I think I would be too worried about injuring him if I timed a tackle wrong! That would be a disaster! I did once get to play against Demetrio Albertini though. He was one of the best midfielders in the world when I was growing up – he won the Champions League with AC Milan. I played against him in midfield in a friendly game. Would you believe me if I told you we won?!

What inspires you to write these books?

When I was younger I wasn't a massive reader. People used to tell me to read all the time but there were no books out there that excited me. They all seemed boring. The Jamie Johnson series is for people out there who are like I was. I try to write the kind of books that I would have been desperate to read.

What's the best game you've ever been to?

In 2002, I was in Japan for the World Cup quarter-final: Brazil v England. It doesn't get much bigger than that!

Jamie Johnson books are often about triumphing over the odds. Can you give us any tips on how to become a professional footballer?

I think it's about your physical and mental dedication. Are you training as hard as you can? Are you working on your weaker foot? Do you believe in yourself? Are you trying to improve every time you play? And, if you get knocked back, how will you react? If you come back stronger, you've got half a chance.

And the other thing to remember is that even if you don't make it as a professional footballer, there are so many other jobs that you can get which involve football. Doctor, physiotherapist, coach, architect... The possibilities are all there, it's a case of going for your goals.

**Want more
thrilling
footballing action?
Catch up on
Jamie Johnson's
journey to the top.**

Jamie Johnson can't believe his luck. He's playing for Kingfield School in a Cup semi-final and scouts from his favourite club, Hawkstone United, are coming to watch!

But Jamie's hopes of a professional career still have a long way to go…

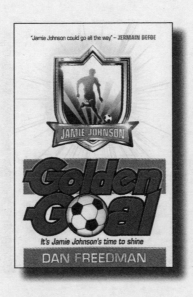

"Jamie Johnson could go all the way" – JERMAIN DEFOE

JAMIE JOHNSON

Golden Goal

It's Jamie Johnson's time to shine

DAN FREEDMAN

There's a huge buzz around Jamie Johnson. He's being talked about as one of the country's most talented young players. But just when he's set for stardom, a shocking event threatens to end his career for ever.

Can Jamie cope with his toughest challenge yet?

"If you like football, this book's for you" – FRANK LAMPARD

JAMIE JOHNSON

Man of the Match

It's crunch time for Jamie Johnson

DAN FREEDMAN

Jamie Johnson is playing the best football of his life for his beloved Hawkstone. But surviving at the top of the league isn't easy. After Hawkstone splash out on a big new signing, Jamie suddenly has a serious rival on the team. And when a series of dramatic events threaten his game, Jamie fears it could all be over…

"World class   genuine world class – that's for ever. Now, the question is: are YOU world class?"

It's the big one! At last, the World Cup beckons for Jamie Johnson. It's the defining moment of his career. But which country will he play for? And will his special skills match up against the greatest players on earth?

This was the team of teams. The club of clubs. And now they wanted him to join them. A transfer to the best club in the world beckons for Jamie Johnson. This is big. This is huge!

However, a time bomb is already ticking within Jamie. . . Is the final whistle about to blow?